# ALL ABOUT HOPE

## ALL OR NOTHING SERIES
### BOOK TWO

## ASHLEY ERIN

*To Andrea.*
*Thank you for your immense support and love for these characters.*
*You have no idea how much it means to me.*

# PROLOGUE

Fall

*Lia*

Music blasts through the dock on the counter, playing the playlist I threw together this afternoon. Dane proposed to Emma this morning and we surprised her with an intimate engagement party. It's now in full swing with champagne flowing. The finger foods disappeared over an hour ago, but when I went to make more I was shuffled away from the fridge and handed a drink.

Emma and Dane are laughing with my parents, while Jesse, Ashton, Ryan, and Alex are huddled near the makeshift bar. Of course, we're all congregated in the kitchen despite my efforts to move the party to the living room. That's just how my family is; besides, I love this kitchen. It's huge.

Pouring myself a fresh glass of champagne, I whistle loudly to get everyone's attention. When all eyes are on me, I lift my glass.

"To Emma and Dane, the two of you fit together like missing pieces of a puzzle. I'm so glad you've found your way to each other.

"Emma, Dane knew early on that you were the one for him. Despite the circumstances that brought you back to us, I'm so glad you're here and officially joining the family. Congrats on your engagement, and I will be eagerly awaiting my Maid of Honor request!" Raising my hand, I fight the tears threatening to fall.

The friend I've always considered more of a sister is glowing, a complete one-eighty to the woman she was only months ago. My pain in the ass brother can't take his eyes off her, their love radiates from them.

She winks at me, mouthing, "I love you." Propping myself onto a bar stool, I sip my champagne as everyone talks over each other. Some may think it is too fast, they've only been together for a few months, but Dane has loved Emma for so long that they couldn't be a better fit. Besides, I've always felt when you know a person is right for you, it doesn't matter how much time passes.

Sighing, I down the rest of my drink and reach over to grasp the near empty bottle of champagne, refilling my glass. Seeing them so happy reminds me how lonely I am. It's self-inflicted, but sometimes I miss the feeling of intimacy and companionship that having a partner or a lover gives. It's been two years, maybe I'm ready to let someone in again.

My eyes are drawn to Alex; they usually are. He's talking to Ryan on the other side of the kitchen, but his eyes are on me. My stomach flutters, anticipation building as we stare at each other. There has been this draw to him since the moment my eyes landed on him four months ago, pissed off and in a state of undress. Smiling to myself as I remember him seething, dragging Dane out of the house, I straighten in my seat as the man who takes up way too much space in my head says something to Ryan and then makes his way towards me.

Standing up and pushing away from the stool, I lean against the counter as he comes to stand next to me. I always feel like I'm more prepared to handle our usual banter when I'm standing. It never goes anywhere, despite my best efforts.

"Take it easy, the night's just beginning." Alex leans in close, his soft cologne enveloping me. Swallowing hard, I shift away trying to ignore the way my body comes to life whenever he's near. The draw I feel terrifies me, and I need some distance so I'm not disappointed when our flirting goes nowhere.

Eyeing him up and down, he looks amazing in dark-wash jeans and a black button-up shirt, I smirk as I take a small sip. "Better?"

His responding grin ignites the small flames in my stomach into a blazing inferno, his smile is one of the things that I find the most attractive about him. And when he looks at me, it widens just a bit showing off his perfect teeth. It's his "Lia" smile, the one I don't think he knows exists. He presses his lips to my ear and says, "Much." Alex straightens to his full height, his arm pressing into mine as we watch our friends celebrating. My body feels like I'm touching a live wire, electricity shooting throughout my limbs. "You look stunning tonight."

Tilting my head up to look at him, the smile forming is unstoppable. The strapless dress is a simple black number, but I almost had to sew it onto my body it's so damn tight. "You're not looking too bad yourself."

Relaxing as we fall into the familiar pattern of shameless flirting, time passes in a blur. I'm exhausted by the time Emma, Dane, Alex, and myself are the only ones remaining in the kitchen. I love my family, but I've been up since five this morning. Glancing at the clock, I groan internally when I see it is two in the morning. I have to be up by six at the latest.

Laughing as Emma shimmies over to me and grabs my hand, I grin at Alex as she spins me in a circle. Her face is flushed with the amount of champagne she has consumed. "Dane and I are leaving, Maid of Honor." Laughing, we hug before they head back over to Emma's house, leaving Alex and me alone.

Glancing at him out of the corner of my eye, I grab a pile of dishes and set them in the sink. I'm too aware of him. He turns off the music, the silence deafening. His hand covers mine as I go to turn on the tap, his body pressing in behind me. My hearts stutters before taking off at a thunderous pace when the heat of his breath teases the sensitive skin below my neck. The only sound in the room is our breathing. It's completely erotic. "What do you think you're doing?" His whisper makes me shiver.

It takes me a moment to respond, my pulse erratic from the feel of his lips on my neck when he spoke, and I know my voice will give away just how much he is impacting me. When I feel under control, I finally open my lips to respond.

"Cleaning up?" Mentally smacking myself, I straighten my body and look at him over my shoulder. Our lips are mere inches apart and my eyes are drawn to his mouth, before flicking back to his laughing hazel eyes. "I wanted to get a head start on cleaning up."

"Leave it, everyone said they would be back to help in the morning." He closes his hand around mine, spinning me to face him. His arms cage me against the counter, my heart pounds in a tremulous rhythm as I search his eyes when he presses his body into mine. We've never crossed any kind of physical boundaries before, and I can't help but hope that he's finally lost control. A control I've been pushing at for months.

The heat that always surrounds us crackles in the air, my breath is coming in short bursts as I watch him war with himself.

Running my hands up his arms, loving the way his muscles move underneath my palms, I wrap my arms around his neck and press my body into his. Tilting my chin up, I look into his eyes and wait for him to decide.

He growls deep in his throat, his eyes flaring. The air whooshes out of me as his lips crash onto mine, devouring me with the hunger of a man who can no longer restrain himself.

# CHAPTER ONE

Spring

*Lia*

Dropping the stack of magazines onto Emma's kitchen counter, I gratefully accept the cup of coffee she thrusts into my hands. Breathing in the comforting aroma, I take an appreciative sip and breathe out a sigh. God, that's good.

"Okay, it's been six months since Dane proposed to you and we have yet to make any real headway, so I'm not leaving here until we at least decide on a venue." Propping myself onto one of the bar stools sitting at her island, I start flipping through one of the magazines. "Why did you want actual magazines? You know you can find all this stuff online, right? Pinterest is a wonderful invention, and it's free."

"I know. I just like the idea of having something to hold in my hands. We can use Pinterest too. And picking a venue is easier said than done, everything around here is booked up so far in advance, and none of it fits us." She sits beside me, leaning in as I pause on a stunning Grecian style wedding dress. "If you ever get married, that style would look incredible on you. Not with your cowboy hat and boots, though. I forbid it."

"Em, we're discussing your actual wedding, not my 'theoretical, probably never gonna happen' wedding." A shadow falls over the counter, drawing our eyes up until we're both looking at Alex. My heart takes off. God, he looks and smells so good.

"Alex, don't you think this dress would look incredible on Lia?" Emma jumps up, giving him a peck on the cheek before topping off her coffee.

He lowers his eyes from where they were locked on mine to the dress on the glossy page. My eyes are drawn to his throat as he swallows before turning away from me and sticking his head in the fridge without answering Emma's question.

Dropping my eyes to the magazine, I casually turn the pages without actually seeing anything. I hate feeling like this. Grabbing my coffee, I down the rest of it to ground myself. I'm not this fucking girl.

"Well?" I tilt my chin up, glaring at Em when she presses, before continuing to flip the pages and ignore the man whose eyes I can feel burning into me. Why bother making eye contact, as soon as I look at him he's just going to look away anyways.

"Lia looks good in anything she wears, so I'm sure she would look beautiful." With that, he leaves the room as quickly as he came in. It's been this way ever since the night we celebrated Emma and Dane's engagement.

The same night we gave in to the heat and had the best sex

I've ever experienced. And sex with Alex is an experience. I haven't been alone in a room with him since then, and I'm not stupid, I know he's avoiding me.

Quite frankly, I'm really pissed off about it. Before that night, we used to have fun together and I feel like I've lost a friend. I thought after the initial awkwardness went away things would get back to normal, but it's still the same. I know he's worried about upsetting me, but the loss of our easy friendship hurts.

"Sorry, Lia, I don't know what his issue is."

I stare at a gorgeous dress, pretending to be immersed in the intricate details of the beads on the bodice as I collect myself before meeting her apologetic gaze. "No worries. Maybe he's just having the world's longest manstruation. We should write in to the Guinness Book of World Records."

Emma throws her head back, her laugh echoing loudly through the kitchen. "He has been excessively moody since we announced our engagement." She frowns, creases marring her forehead. "It's probably not easy for him. For so long, we only had each other, now he knows I don't need him in quite the same way. He can't hide behind me anymore, using me as an excuse to not look for something more in his life than work and our friendship."

"Do you think he has feelings for you?"

Almost falling out of her chair at that, Emma's laughs wrack her body to the point I'm worried she's going to hurt herself. "Oh my God, NO. Gross. He's as much a brother to me as Dane and Ryan are to you. The same goes for the way he looks at me. There has never even been an inkling. That would just be wrong."

Even though I knew this, I'm still relieved. Emma continues to ponder what could be bothering him as we mark pages that we like in the wedding magazines. I feel guilty for not opening up to her, but it was a one-night thing. Clearly, since Alex can't even be in the same room as me. The heat between us has only escalated for me since that night, the ache in my body for the pleasure of his touch flaring every time we lock eyes, but apparently one time was enough for him.

Actually, I don't think that's true. I can read him pretty well, I think he's scared of letting someone in. Letting something meaningful develop, but I never said I wanted anything more from him. And now that night haunts my dreams. A constant reminder of something in my life that I had momentarily let myself hope that one night would become more.

Trying to shake thoughts of my non-existent "whatever" with Alex, I force myself to focus instead on my best friend. This afternoon is about her.

Closing my eyes, I try to picture the perfect place for her and Dane to get married. It needs to be close to home and rustic. It should be open, and we should have the ability to decorate it however we want.

The list of places available disappears rapidly as I ponder what they would like, until one glaringly obvious option remains. *Why didn't I think of this before?*

"Em, I'm a fucking genius! What if we cover the sand in the large arena and decorate it with flowers, lights, and whatever other decorations you decide you want. It's rustic, we know there's enough room, and then there is no rush to clean up the space after, plus you don't have to book it ridiculously far in advance, so you can have the wedding whenever you want."

She closes the magazine she is flipping through with a slap of her hand. "Why didn't I think of that? It's brilliant! All of the places we've been looking at are booking over a year from now. I don't want to wait that long." Leaning over, she wraps her arm around my shoulders, squeezing.

"I'm not always just a hat rack." Laughing, I pull a notepad over and we start sketching ideas, and jotting notes about decorations.

Ollie runs to the end of the arena, waiting for my cue. Kicking my heels out, I say, "Whoa." He slides to a stop, the tracks he's left behind are straight and true.

After leaving Emma's house an hour ago, I desperately needed to get my mind off weddings, and relationships, and stupid men who fuck me and then avoid me after giving me a taste of something I forgot I desperately needed.

So, I saddled Ollie and have been going through some reining patterns. Show season is upon us, the first in just over a month, and I want to be sure we're ready.

Lifting my right rein, I roll my spur into his left flank. He spins on the spot, the room around us blurring with the speed of the spin. Stopping him, I let him rest a moment before lifting my left rein and this time rolling my spur into his right flank. He spins in the opposite direction, the tightness of the circle envied by many.

Ollie is eight years old and has been my reining horse since we entered the Futurity, the chance for first time reining horses to show what they have and win big, when he was three years old. In the five years I've had him, the bond we've formed is envied both in and out of the arena. He will be with me until the day he dies, despite offers of tens of thousands of dollars to buy him.

Patting Ollie on his neck, I frown when I see Alex through the large windows at the end of the arena. Everything I've been trying to clear my head of comes back with a vengeance. It really bothers me that Alex initiated what happened that night, and then proceeded to avoid me like I'm a carrier of the plague.

I didn't ask him to pin me against the counter and kiss me with an explosive passion that still has my body thrumming six months later. Nor did I ask him to wrap my legs around his waist and fuck me until I had the most earth shattering orgasm I've ever experienced.

Growling, I nudge Ollie into a canter, circling the arena working on lead changes until we are both covered in a sheen of sweat. I love the speed of this sport, and the connection between horse and rider. It's a testament to how frustrated I am that I don't feel better after a solid hour of working.

Slowing Ollie to a trot, I begin our cooldown. When his breathing has slowed, I dismount and walk him around the arena a couple times to ensure he's cooled down enough. Leading him to the tie stall, I quickly untack him and rub him down until his coat shines before settling him into his stall with some feed and his supplements. The entire time I perform my tasks, I'm remembering that night with such acuity that by the time I'm done putting his tack away, my body is quivering in need.

Scowling, I clench my thighs trying to alleviate the ache, getting more and more pissed off at Alex the entire time. He did this to me. I was fine. I met my own needs and didn't need anything from anyone. Now, I can't come unless it's to images in my head of that night with Alex. He's ruined my ability to need nothing from anyone.

Flipping the lights, I burst through the door cursing under my breath and crash into a hard, hot body. Glancing up, I step back into the now closed door of the barn. "Alex."

Alex's hazel eyes take in my disheveled appearance. My hair is wild from running patterns with Ollie, my skin covered in a light layer of sweat and dust. When his eyes fall on the slight sliver of skin showing between my jeans and tank top, his eyes shoot back to mine where they bore into my soul. He steps back a foot, his eyes moving between mine and the barn door as he tries to think of something to say. "I didn't know you were in the barn."

"I was working Ollie. We have a show in May." Tucking my hands in my back pockets, I lean back, propping one foot against the wall, trying to ignore the way my body has lit up from the inside. I've spent the last ninety minutes replaying that one night, and now the object of my desire is standing here looking at me with false indifference. Despite his best efforts, I know he's still attracted to me, because if he wasn't, he wouldn't be avoiding me all of the damn time.

When he starts to turn without another word, I shove off the wall, closing the distance between us.

Enough is enough.

I fist my hand in his shirt when he moves to walk away again, and step into him, tilting my head up so he can't avoid looking at me. "You've been avoiding me."

"No . . ." He tries to look away, but I raise my other hand and hold it against the back of his head.

"Don't lie to me, Alex. We used to spend time together, and now you don't remain in a room with me more than the necessary amount of time to be considered polite. Don't even get me started on the fact you haven't been alone with me since the engagement party.

"What I don't get is that you're the one who initiated that night. You're the one who made the first move, not me. I haven't been some clingy chick you picked up in a bar, so what gives?" Holding him in place, I glare up at him, locking his gaze in mine.

He sighs and runs a hand down his face before looking at

my hand still grasping his shirt. "I've been a dick for no reason, haven't I?"

"Well, I wasn't going to use those exact words, but yeah." Grinning, I drop my hand when he chuckles softly.

"In the heat of the moment, all I could think about was you and how much I wanted to feel you. Afterwards, all I could think about was everyone else and what they would do if they found out. I don't want a relationship and the pressure would be there, I know how Emma thinks." His smirk drops into a frown as I gape at him.

"That is the lamest thing I've ever heard. Your hot factor just dropped by two points." Crossing my arms over my chest, I narrow my eyes. His Adam's apple bobs as he swallows, but there is a slight smirk he's fighting at my comment. Cocking my hip out, I scowl. "Let's go through these one at a time. First off, no one knows what happened and there is no reason for them to know. Second, you're assuming I want a relationship; that's something I haven't had the desire for in a long time. Been there, done that, and I have the emotional scarring as a souvenir."

Alex has made me wonder, hope even, but for the most part I'm still leery of entering a relationship, especially with someone as skittish as Alex, so I don't feel like I'm lying.

"My hot factor?" Alex grins at me, cocking his head to the side in a way that is too cute. He's trying to distract me, but it won't work.

"Seriously? That's what you took from that?" Shaking my head, I step toward him and place my hand on his chest, pressing my body into his. For a moment, all I can think about is the hard muscle beneath my hand and remembering the way it looked when he pounded into me.

Grinding my teeth, I focus back on the man before me. "All I want is someone I trust to have hot sex with. Get your head out of your ass and think about it. If that's not what you want, fine, but we're friends Alex, and it hurts my feelings that it's so easy for you to forget that."

Lifting onto my toes, I press a chaste kiss to his lips, drawing away before he can react. Brushing past him, I saunter to my house.

I'm not a pushover, and I'm not going to let him get away with this shitty behavior any more.

# CHAPTER TWO

*Alex*

I slept like complete and utter shit last night. Tossing and turning as I replayed Lia's taunt in my head, I'm guessing I got no more than three hours. Three hours that were filled with dreams of Lia beneath me. Not that those dreams are anything new, I've had them every night since Emma and Dane's engagement party.

Her words are on repeat in my head.

*You're avoiding me.*

*I'm not some clingy chick you picked up in a bar.*

*We're friends . . .*

*You hurt my feelings.*

As if I'm not already haunted by that one night, her slender body pressed against mine as I pounded into her tight, wet pussy, but now the guilt I've been ignoring at the way I've been avoiding her is at the forefront of my mind.

Throwing the covers off, I sit on the edge of my bed,

running my hands down my face. For months Lia allowed me to avoid her, but she's made it clear she's not willing to play that game anymore.

I've never been a coward, but I've also never been attracted to someone so close to Emma before. All of my previous partners have been strangers I've picked up—typical one-night stands. The closest I had to a serious relationship was a similar arrangement to what Lia is suggesting, but six months in she couldn't handle my friendship with Emma so I was done. Lia is part of Emma's family, which means I need to tread carefully. Although, at least I can be sure she won't get jealous of Em.

"Alex, are you coming?" Emma knocks on the door, opening it after a beat.

"Yeah." Tugging the t-shirt I'm holding over my head, I follow her out of my room and down the stairs. Chloe is bouncing around at our feet, a toy in her mouth. Stepping onto the porch, I throw it for her, my eyes on the house across the yard.

"You seem distracted. Are you finally going to tell me what's gotten your panties in a bunch for the past six months?" Emma bends to take the toy from Chloe and throws it for her again.

"I'm fine, really." Avoiding Emma's look of disbelief, I watch Chloe play by herself in the yard.

"You're so full of shit." She bounds down the steps, shaking her head. "It's me, we've been telling each other everything for a decade. Now stop being avoidant."

Lengthening my strides, I catch up to her and glance down. Her feelings are hurt, the look on her face makes my stomach twist. I'm on a fucking roll.

"I'm sorry, it's not that I want to keep anything from you, I just don't know how to put it into words." The lie comes easily,

I've been saying it enough over the past several months. She looks at me skeptically, but accepts my answer.

As we walk into the Hyatt's house, I shove my thumbs into the pocket of my jeans.

I hate that I've been so fucking moody. It changes now, I'm not this guy.

Walking into the kitchen, I fight the grin that threatens when I see the only available seats are next to Lia and Dane. She's really not going to let me avoid this anymore.

"Good morning." Filling my plate, I listen to Ryan and Dane discussing the horses. The mares in foal are due in about a month and they're moving them closer to the house today to prepare.

"Alex, if you're free, we could use an extra hand," Ryan inquires.

"Yeah, I would . . ." My cutlery clatters to my plate as a hand strokes over my cock, gripping me through my jeans. Five sets of eyes watch me as I adjust the table cloth, and clear my throat. "Yeah, I would be glad to help."

Swallowing hard, I pick up my knife and fork, shrugging innocently at Emma's glance before I look sideways at Lia. The smirk on her face as she eats is a silent challenge.

Ryan and Dane return to their conversation, leaving me to try and act like nothing out of the ordinary is going on.

Cutting into my French toast, I focus on chewing, the normally delicious meal has no flavor. Every part of my body is zoned in on Lia stroking me and trying to act as though I don't have an erection at the breakfast table.

Forcing my face into a look of passiveness, I tune back into the conversation Dane and Ryan are having, hoping to distract myself. They're now discussing the yearlings and which ones they want to sell.

"Alex, I want to add photos of some of the yearlings to the

ranch's website. Do you have time to sit down this week and tweak it a little bit?" Dane looks over at me and I'm glad I've been paying attention to more than the hand that has now made its way *inside* my boxer briefs.

"Yeah, that shouldn't be a problem." My voice is low and I fight a groan as Lia's thumb teases the tip of my dick before stroking down in a slow torturous motion.

"Perfect. I will take some photos after we move the mares today and email them to you later. The layout is perfect, I was thinking we should separate the horses by age and the amount of training they've had, rather than have them all on the same page. If we can create a tab that appears when you hover the mouse over the sale button, I think that would be perfect."

Nodding in response, I quickly stuff a forkful of food into my mouth to keep a groan from escaping. Lia's hand has picked up the pace, stroking me in exactly the way I like it.

Lia chuckles softly to herself as she slides her hand out of my pants and stands up from the table, carrying her dishes to the sink. My eyes follow her as she first rinses then sticks them in the dishwasher, before walking to the door of the kitchen.

"Well, friends, I'm off to the clinic." She winks at me with a smirk before walking out of the room, everyone saying casual goodbyes and chatting, all the while I'm trying not to chase after her. My dick screams at her for leaving me like this, an ache already forming from the absence of release. She will be punished for this.

Releasing the mare from her halter, I watch as she trots off to the fresh round bale of hay Jesse dropped in the pen after breakfast this morning. Pulling the baseball cap off my head, I swipe my hand across my forehead before replacing it.

Dane and Ryan have fifteen horses in foal, all due within a couple weeks of each other. I missed seeing the foals being born last year, arriving on the ranch when they were already almost two months old. I've learned that in the horse world, they prefer foals to be born in May. I don't really understand the reason behind it, but seasonally it makes sense. The snow is finally gone and the weather is warming up.

"Is there anything else I can help you with?" Turning away from the horses, I look to the guys.

Dane latches the gate before facing me, shaking his head. "No. Ryan has to head out to a client's house, and I have six horses I need to work today. Thanks for your help with these mares, it saved us an extra trip."

Nodding, we say goodbye and I head to the small barn on Emma's land. Grabbing my saddle, I set out to get Chandler ready. Lia is going to learn what happens when she taunts me.

All morning I've been distracted, trying to decide how to repay her for what she did at the breakfast table. It's clear that the sexual tension between us is only growing, so I'm giving in to what we both want.

The ride to Lia's clinic seems to take twice as long as usual. The state of art building is massive. It has its own entrance from the road, so clients don't infringe on the family's private space.

Lia's half of the building features six indoor stalls, a tie stall, a wash stall, a small arena, and a pool that is specially built for horses. Off to the side is her office, which also houses a small living quarters for nights she needs to stay close to her patients.

Ryan's half of the building is smaller. It's one open room that has all the supplies he needs for his clients, including space to work on horses in the rare occasion a client travels to him. The Hyatt's ranch is immensely successful, and they work hard to maintain the buildings and land.

Glancing around, I see that Ryan's work truck isn't in its usual place, the windows of his shop dark. Thankfully, most of his work is done at his clients' houses, which makes it easier for me to see Lia without worrying about interruptions.

Dismounting, I tie Chandler in one of the tie stalls attached to the building, tossing him some hay from the stack alongside it. The door to Lia's clinic is open, a dance song I don't recognize drifting out. Lia is facing away from the door, shaking her hips as she fills in the giant calendar on her wall.

Leaning against the doorframe, I take in the view, a grin growing on my face. She is barefoot, her boots lying next to the open door. Her dark hair falls in loose waves over her shoulders, and, at some point, she changed from her jeans into a flowing skirt that brushes the tops of her knees. Perfect.

Lia spins in a circle, her skirt swirling out to reveal her toned legs. Legs that I can't wait to have wrapped around me again.

Her eyes widen and she stumbles when she catches sight of me in the doorway before bending over laughing. "Oh my God. You scared the crap out of me, you creeper." She straightens her body, dropping down into her office chair, soft chuckles drawing my eyes to the low V of her tank top.

Dragging my gaze from the flush on her chest, I finally look into her eyes, smirking when I see a hint of hesitation. She's apprehensive and she should be. Pushing away from the doorway, shutting it with a kick behind me, I slowly walk towards her. "I thought it was time for you to be punished for this morning."

Her eyes lighten with amusement as she leans back in her chair, crossing her ankles underneath her. Her warm brown eyes focus on each movement I make, they glow with a challenge that I'm eager to meet. She hums as I get closer, the sound sending a bolt of arousal down my spine and straight to my cock.

I move around her desk and drop to my knees before her without losing eye contact. Biting back a groan at the look of heated interest, I slide my hands under her skirt, grab her panties and tug them down her legs. She lifts her hips without me asking, her hands gripping the arm rests of her chair.

I shift her forward, bunching her skirt up around her hips. "You're so beautiful." Trailing my fingertips over her pussy, I groan at how wet she is. "You're so wet for me and I haven't even done anything yet."

"If this is your form of punishment, feel free to punish me any time you want." Her eyes drift closed as I increase the pressure, her words coming out on a moan as I slide one finger into her wet heat.

Grinning, I pull my hand away until she opens her eyes and glares at me. Leaning forward, I slide my tongue over her, watching her face as she shifts closer to me. Her eyes are hooded, but she doesn't close them again, instead she watches me as I start to devour her.

I work her clit with my tongue as I slide two fingers into her, curling them to hit that sweet spot. Her moans get louder as I consume her, my tongue circling her nub as I work my fingers faster until she's shaking. Her body tenses as she pushes into me.

"God, you're so fucking responsive." Watching her, I throw away my plan to leave her aching like she did to me. She's too beautiful and I've been haunted by the singular vision I have of her orgasming. I need to see it again.

I've never been with a woman like Lia. She's not afraid to demand more of me, but her body tells me exactly what she needs. I want to learn every sweet spot. I want to hear her scream my name. I just want more of her.

"Alex . . ."

"I know, baby." She's so close. Sucking on her clit, I pump my fingers faster bringing her there when a knock interrupts us.

Lia frantically shoves me under her desk, much to my amusement, before straightening her skirt and opening her laptop. "Yeah?" Her voice is hoarse, thick with need.

"Hey." Dane's voice is unmistakable, even muffled by the large desk I'm huddled under. "Where is Alex?"

Lia coughs, shifting her chair closer to the desk. "Alex? I have no idea, why?"

Her voice cracks, and as much as I'm enjoying this, it's also tempting me to play dirty. I don't want Dane to know I'm here, but an opportunity has presented itself to tease Lia.

"Oh. Chandler is tied up outside, since Ryan isn't here I just assumed he was in here with you." Grinning at the skepticism in his voice, I hold in a laugh as Lia squirms in her chair. Forcing her knees open with my shoulder, I slide my hand under her skirt and up her thigh, circling her clit with my thumb as she sputters out a response.

"Maybe he wanted to see the yearlings and didn't want to risk Chandler getting overly excited." She tries to shove my hand away. Instead, I lean in and fuck her with my tongue, increasing the pressure of my thumb. Lia's hand fists in my hair, pulling it as she clears her throat. "Anyways, I really need to finish up what I'm working on."

"You're being weird. What's going on?" His voice gets closer as he moves into the room.

She tries to push me away with her hands, while her hips shift even closer. Her voice is strangled when she says, "Nothing. I just need to be alone." Her voice squeaks over the last word as I increase the pace of my tongue. I can feel her body shivering, getting closer to release and I relentlessly devour her.

"Okay . . ." He drags out the word, clearly not believing her. "Emma and I are hosting game night tonight at Emma's house. Are you interested in joining us?"

"Sounds fun." Lia's voice is tight, her legs shaking, her body tensing as she tries to hold back her orgasm.

"Eight o'clock." Dane walks back across the room, the door shutting behind him.

Lia collapses onto her arms on the desk as I suck on her clit, her cries muffled as her release wracks her body. When she quiets, I push her chair back, and crawl out from under the desk. She leans back weakly, watching me. Bending down, I brace myself on the arms of her chair, caging her in. Capturing her lips with mine, I kiss her with the pent up desire I've been holding in for the past six months.

Her hands grip my shoulders as she opens up to me, allowing my tongue to fuck her mouth until we're both gasping for air.

"Okay, let's try this. No strings. No one knows but us. If it gets too complicated, we just end it. No harm, no foul." Searching her eyes for any hesitation, relief floods me when all I see is heat. "We're friends first and I don't want to lose that, or hurt you any more than I have."

"Agreed." She tilts her head up, kissing me one last time before pushing me away. "Okay, I really do have work I need to finish. See you tonight."

Winking at her, I can't wipe the smile off my face as I untie Chandler and swing up into the saddle.

# CHAPTER THREE

*Lia*

Ryan and I let ourselves into Emma's house, following the sound of laughter to her kitchen. The granite counter is covered with finger foods, the island made into a bar, but our appreciation of the delectable array before us is short-lived when we both see Dane.

His face is covered in whipped cream, while Alex and Emma laugh at him.

"Did we miss a food fight?" Ryan chuckles as Dane scowls at him. Grinning, I grab a towel and run it under the tap. I need time to compose myself before I face him.

"Emma thought it would be fucking hilarious to smash whipped cream all over me."

"I wish I had my camera." Laughing, I regret leaving my cell at home.

He takes the damp towel I hand to him, wiping his face off

with a scowl that is completely nullified by the laughter in his eyes.

Taking the goblet Emma hands to me, I pour myself a glass of red wine.

Sipping it, I glance at Alex over the rim, smiling when he winks at me. He looks delicious in jeans and a plain black t-shirt that hugs his muscles. I haven't gotten to explore them thoroughly yet, our previous dalliance hot and rushed, but I've been fantasizing about all the dirty things I plan on doing to him. Licking my lips, I run my eyes over him once more before returning his heated gaze with a sly smile.

"It's just us tonight. Ashton has a date and Jesse is sulking at home." Dane sits down at the table, a deck of cards sitting in the center and begins shuffling. "He got pretty pissed off at me when I tried to help."

"Telling him he needs to pull his head out of his ass isn't helping." Emma looks over at me, "Men, right?"

Chuckling, I nod. "Yeah. Sometimes you can't fix things, big brother."

Alex, Ryan, and Dane all scowl at the implication they can't fix any problem. Em and I burst out laughing, they kind of look like petulant children who aren't allowed a second scoop of ice cream.

Leaning over the counter, I chew on my lip as I decide what to start with. The puff pastry spinach cheese swirls look to die for, so I place a few on my plate before loading the rest with veggies and a homemade ranch dip.

With one last look at the food, I sit at the table on the empty seat next to Alex as Dane deals out the cards. Alex brushes his hand over my hip before picking up his cards, leaving a trail of tingles.

"Who wants to bet on their ability to beat me today?" Peeking at the front two cards, I look around the table.

"Nah." Ryan shakes his head as he arranges his cards on the table.

Smirking, "Aww, poor big brother doesn't want to empty his wallet again?"

"Not really, I just dropped fifteen grand today so I just don't have that much left over to spare." We all gape at Ryan as he snatches a carrot from my plate. He looks around at our faces and grins.

"On what?"

"It's always been the plan for you to keep the main house, Dane's stuff is all moved over here now, so I thought it was time to build my own home. I've been meeting with contractors and signed the papers this morning. We're breaking ground as soon as possible."

I feel the familiar prick of tears and drop my head so no one sees them. I'm so used to having my brothers around all the time, hearing them in the house moving around, that the idea of being there alone fills me with a sense of emptiness.

Everyone is moving forward with their lives, and I'm in the same place I have been for the past two and a half years. Too stubborn to move forward with anything other than my business.

"Oh."

Ryan turns me to face him. "Hey. What's this?"

Shrugging, I blink a few times until my sight clears. "I guess I just like having you around. Who would've thought that was possible?"

"You're stuck with me for a while yet, besides it's not like I'm going far. I'm building next to the clinic, where I've always planned." He pinches my chin and grins at me. "I love you, too, sis."

Leaning into him, I shove aside my moment of weakness, glancing at the man on my other side. The warmth of his gaze as he smiles at me holds a promise for later. That thought makes me feel better, so I straighten and shake off the moment of doubt.

"Okay, so how do we play this game?" Alex chimes in, bringing us back to why we're here.

"It's called Golf. The point of the game is to get to zero points. Arrange your four cards in a square, face down, two on top and two on the bottom. You can look at the bottom two cards now, but memorize them because you can't peek again. Kings are zero, Aces are one, and the rest follow their numbers.

"At the beginning of your turn you draw a card, or take the one the person before you discarded. The goal is to swap cards until your overall score is a zero or as low as you can get it. If you get a pair, they cancel each other out to create a zero. When you hit a low number, or zero, knock and then on your next turn everyone has to flip their cards." I explain the game as I look at the bottom two cards before me. Fighting a grin when I see a King and a two.

"Don't let that innocent face fool you." Dane points at me with a potato chip in his hand. "Lia has ridiculous luck with this game. I started with two Kings once, so I figured I had a good chance of winning. I bet Lia a hundred bucks I would beat her. I lost." Dane shakes his head, grimacing when he recalls counting out five twenties as I danced around the kitchen.

Alex grins at me, his eyes dancing with humor. "A bit of a card shark are you?"

Shrugging, "I played during the lunch hour with my friends when I was in school. One time..."

"At band camp?" Emma interrupts, laughing.

"At Tony Zimmerman's, we were playing strip poker."

Dane and Ryan groan, glaring at me. Smirking, I continue my story.

"Anyways, by the time the game finished, I was the only

one fully dressed. It was fantastic." Leaning back in my chair, I wink at Emma. "Do you remember meeting Tony?"

"Is he the one with . . . ?"

"Yep." We burst out laughing as the guys shake their heads.

"We don't want to know." Ryan and Dane say in unison.

We're going around the table, drawing cards and swapping. Two rounds in and I've already reached zero, but I hold out a couple rounds to let them get their hopes up.

Alex leans into me. "What did he have?"

"A magic tongue. Well, that's what the rumor mill said anyways, and by the size and length of his tongue I can believe it." Alex looks like he regrets asking as he draws a card and swaps out one of his top two cards.

When it's finally my turn, I look around the table and knock. A chorus of groans erupts around me as we circle the table one more time.

"Can't we play Pictionary? At least we all have a fighting chance with that one," Dane grumbles when we all turn over our cards. I'm impressed to see Alex only has two points.

"Don't be a sore loser." My tone is smug, causing him to throw popcorn at me with a ridiculous pout on his face. "I'm guessing we're going the full eighteen holes?"

"Like you would agree to any less," Dane mumbles. Chuckling, I roll my eyes at him.

Ryan gets up to grab some food and pour himself a drink while Emma shuffles the cards. Alex shifts in his seat, his movement causing his arm to brush against mine, sending tingles straight to the ache in my lower belly.

My whole body has been on high alert since I came at my desk this afternoon. Being near him has my body begging for more, my panties are wet and my pussy is aching to feel him inside me again.

Clenching my thighs, I arrange the cards and look at the

bottom two. This hand isn't a good start, but I have no doubt I can make it work in my favor.

Several rounds in, I excuse myself to go to the bathroom. After washing my hands, I open the door to see Alex leaning against the wall. He pushes me back into the small room, shutting the door behind me.

Our bodies crash into each other, his lips moving against mine. When he lifts me, I wrap my legs around him and press my center into him.

His lips trail from my lips to my neck, sending fire through my veins.

Reluctantly, he lowers me to the ground.

"Crap, we better get back out there." He runs a hand over his jaw, looking at me like he wants to carry me upstairs and finish what we've started. "Too bad you're set on playing the full game."

He kisses me once more, before leaving the bathroom.

By the time we call it a night, I'm on fire. Accidental touches here and there kept my body extremely aware of Alex. That and the promise of what's to come, I'm so distracted I've almost lost a couple of rounds.

Ryan and I close the door to the house, heading upstairs in silence.

With a goodnight, I watch the door to his room close before shutting myself in my bedroom. I quickly grab my phone to text Alex.

Me: Be here in 30 minutes.

Alex: Nothing can stop me.

Ryan's door is closed, his lights out. Creeping down the stairs, I open the door to Alex. He's changed into sweats, causing my heart to flutter wildly when I see how aroused he is. Grabbing his shirt, I yank him inside and shut the door a little too hard.

Alex freezes, but I know Ryan is out like a light for the night. Lifting onto my toes, I brush my lips against his, pulling away before he can deepen the kiss.

Turning on my heel, I saunter up the steps, looking over my shoulder at him as I pull my tank top over my head and throw it at him.

His eyes heat, and he starts taking the stairs two at a time, stalking me into my bedroom. We make quick work of our clothes, tumbling onto my bed in a tangle of limbs and desperate passion.

Alex pins my arms above my head, leaning down to nip my lips. I hate being restrained. It's something I used to love, giving up control to someone you trust implicitly, but Alex hasn't earned that trust yet, maybe never. Wrapping my legs around his waist, I grind against the head of his cock, using his surprise to free my arms.

Tightening my legs, I grip his ass and pull him into me, reveling in the way my body stretches to accommodate him.

"Fuck, Lia, you're so tight. You feel amazing." Alex's voice is raspy with need, his arms tight from where he braces above me trying to hold himself back.

"I need you to move. Now." Shifting my hips, I dig my fingers into the hard muscles of his ass, silently begging him.

He smirks down at me, moving slowly out of me before thrusting back in. Hard.

"God, yes," I moan. "Harder."

I lift my hips to meet each thrust, loving the way the pleasure borders on painful, but in a way I didn't know I needed. He drops to his elbows, kissing me as he twists his hips into mine causing me to clench around him. I can feel my orgasm building, my body overwhelmed with all of the sensations. His tongue strokes mine as he deepens the kiss before pulling away and reaching down to circle my clit with two fingers.

"Let go, baby." He pulls out and thrusts into me as he increases the pressure on my clit. My body shatters into a million different sensations as I pulse around him. He stills inside me as he finds his own release, the force of our orgasms is overwhelming and if I could, I would look anywhere but into his eyes. His hands hold my head still as he looks down at me, before softly brushing his lips over mine.

Alex moves to lay next to me, his hand drawing soft circles on my stomach, his lips trailing soft kisses over my neck and shoulders. I can't stop the shivers his teasing causes, and feel him grin against my skin.

"I couldn't wait to be inside of you, the past six months have been brutal. But now I'm going to worship every inch of your gorgeous body until you're quaking beneath me and begging me to let you come." He lowers his head and wraps his lips around a nipple, sucking hard. My back bows up off the bed, whispery moans escaping from my throat.

He has no idea what his touch does to me, my body is already begging him for more.

# CHAPTER FOUR

*Lia*

Pacing my clinic, I stare at my cell phone, the text I've typed out is taunting me. Flipping it so it's face down, I go back to cleaning my already spotless office. It's been two days since game night at Emma's. Two days since Alex and I spent the night familiarizing ourselves with each other.

We've seen each other since then, our easy friendship returning, but I've resisted the temptation to summon him for some much needed friends-with-benefits action. We never really established any rules, aside from not telling anyone and not allowing it to interfere with our friendship.

*Just press send.*

Staring at where I left my phone, I walk over and send the text. No turning back. Nothing has changed, but I chew on the inside of my cheek as doubt fills me.

"Everything will be great. Positivity, Lia. You're good at that." *Oh great, now I'm talking to myself.* We've agreed to this arrangement, it doesn't matter who initiates, but I can't help the knot in my stomach. This is asking more of him than just sex, this is giving him the power to see me vulnerable, and I hate losing control.

The sound of horses whinnying outside distracts me from the swirling vortex of doubt I'm being sucked into. Shutting down my computer, I lock up and head outside, grateful for a distraction. I need to get out of my head.

Alex greets me from where his sits atop Chandler, his lips breaking into a wide smile as I gape up at him, shocked that he is here to see me. "Want to go for a ride?" Following the gesture of his hand, I see Ollie is already saddled and ready to go.

Searching his face, I'm relieved to see he's relaxed and happy, the heat in his eyes as he scans them over my body unravels the tightness in my stomach and replaces it with a delicious ache. Figures, I worked myself up over nothing. Relaxing, I walk over to Ollie.

"What would you do if I said no?" Sliding my foot into the stirrup, I step up into the saddle and grin at him.

Shrugging, he teases back. "I guess you will have to say no to find out."

He turns Chandler and leads the way down one of the many trails crisscrossing throughout my family's ranch.

"How was your day?" Sinking into the saddle, I lose myself in the comfort of being on horseback. I've been on horseback since I was an infant, riding with my parents, and then by myself as soon as I was capable of staying in the saddle. Being here feels as natural as breathing.

"Good, I finished updating the website for Dane. I had no idea he was going to sell so many of the foals. It makes sense, I guess, but I would have a hard time choosing." He's been learning a lot from Dane as they build the ranch's website. He built mine and Ryan's from scratch, and they're absolutely perfect. He took what Dane had for the rest of the ranch, and made major changes so it is now user friendly and easy to find.

"That's why Dane is in charge of the sales aspect of the ranch. I would keep them all and that's not realistic." Falling silent, the wind rustles the new green of the leaves. I love the spring. The shift in the weather from freezing to cool to warm. The new growth of plants, and the freshness in the air. There is something beautiful in how Mother Nature goes through her cycles, each one bringing renewal to the earth.

The bright green of new leaves creates a vibrant background as we ride. Breathing deeply, I focus on Alex leading the way through the trails. Change has been a huge part of our lives this year. Emma returned home and the change in her has been substantial.

The man in front of me has grown more comfortable with ranch life, his enjoyment of horses and eagerness to learn shining through. He is always so cheerful and up front, it's refreshing. When I think about his smile and how contagious it is, it hurts my heart to know that beneath it is a man scared to attach to people. Emma told me about when he used to sneak into her room, covered in bruises and burn marks.

How anyone, especially the woman who gave birth to him, could do that to him is beyond me. He is the type of person that warms those around him. He's the type of man I used to dream about when I was a teenager.

He cares so deeply once he allows himself to. I wonder if that's why he didn't respond to my text. It's asking him to care more than he's ready for.

Watching him as he rides, my stomach clenches at the way the muscles in his back flex as he shifts in the saddle. It's a testament to how vulnerable I feel, that I'm not more distracted by how sexy he looks sitting in the saddle with a confidence that wasn't there not too long ago.

"Dane offered to let me choose one of the yearlings. I thought maybe you could help me pick." Alex looks over at me, his question hanging in the air as I return from my thoughts. "If you're not too worn out from my phenomenal sex skills that is." He smirks as I roll my eyes.

"I'm going to ignore that and focus on the first part of your statement. Let me think on the horses so I pick the right one. Dane and I can help you train it, I want you to do the work, but we will be there." His smile lights up his face.

"I have a question and maybe I should be embarrassed, but I have no shame. Why are there three words for a baby horse?" He cocks his eyebrow at me causing me to throw my head back and laugh. His facial expression is ridiculous and it takes me a moment to focus on his question.

"Foal is gender neutral whereas a filly refers to a girl and colt refers to a boy."

"I think I knew that."

"Then why did you ask?"

"Why not? Besides, you looked stuck in your head and sometimes that's not a good place to be." He turns Chandler to head towards home, silently waiting for my reply.

"Why didn't you answer my text?" Blurting the words out, instead of feeling embarrassed, I just feel relieved to voice the question that's been turning around in my brain since I sent it. Alex is usually quick to respond, and he hasn't mentioned it.

"I left my phone at home, the battery died while I was working. What did your text say?"

Crap. "An old friend of mine, Lydia, has a horse that's been injured and she's decided to come to me instead of going elsewhere."

"Okay." He looks over his shoulder at me, confused.

"She's the woman I caught having sex with Graham, my ex. The same woman who is still with him. I texted hoping maybe you could be there, for moral support."

"Of course I will be there." The tenseness I didn't realize I was holding leaves my body and I sigh. Having him there will make it so much easier.

"So . . . What brought on this impromptu ride?" The trail widens and I nudge Ollie to catch up so we can ride alongside each other.

His lips tilt up as though my curiosity amuses him. "I like you for more than what your body does to me, Lia. I missed talking with you while I had my head shoved up my ass. I want the *friends* part of this as much as the *benefits* part."

Grinning, I can't stop the internal swooning from happening. The Lia in my head does a happy dance, complete with a backflip that in real life would break my head.

"You know you look fucking sexy sitting in that saddle." Lowering my voice, I ask Ollie to stop as I reach my hand up and start teasing the dip in my shirt that shows off my cleavage.

Alex's eyes follow the movement, before looking around, scanning the area. We're close to the house, but silence surrounds us. He swings off Chandler, tying him to a tree, before dragging me off Ollie. "It's amazing how graceful you look, even when being removed from your horse."

Suddenly finding myself on my back, Alex's hips rocking into mine, I moan as the pressure builds between my legs. "Is friend time over?" My voice is husky, my eyes heavy with arousal as he inches down my body.

Lifting my hips as he ignores my question, his hands remove my jeans and thong in one swift motion. My head ignores the possibility of being caught when he buries his face between my legs.

"You have no idea how beautiful you are. So perfect and ready for me." His tongue strokes me in long, slow motions, before delving into me on a groan. I push myself more firmly against his mouth, feeling no shame in asking for more.

His tongue strokes me, pressing all the right buttons and hitting spots that make my ears ring. Alex's stubble scratches my skin increasing my sensitivity and it doesn't take long for my body to start contracting, pleasure pulsing through my extremities as his tongue brings me to my climax.

Alex leans back on his heels, licking his lips before smirking. Standing, he lifts me off the ground, kissing me with force and passion, my taste still on his lips. "I love the way you taste." He presses back into me, hands wrapped around the small of my back as his lips move over mine with the perfect amount of pressure. Too soon he pulls away, handing me my jeans before untying the horses.

My legs are shaking so I lean against a tree to get support in redressing. My mind is a jumbled, gooey mess so I don't bother responding, focusing instead on straightening my clothes and picking twigs out of my hair.

Ollie snorts as I hop back in the saddle, less gracefully than normal and kick him into a trot, leading Alex out of the woods and towards the barn.

We break through the tree line, the horses eager to get to their pens and eat. Chandler starts trotting towards his girls when he sees Emma pitching hay over the fence. Alex looks over at me, winking as he leads Chandler over to be untacked and fed.

Instead of turning Ollie out, I lead him to the outdoor arena to work him a bit. He's had a few days off and the ride with Alex was a good warm up.

Ryan is by the gate to the arena and lets me in, leaning against the fence watching me as I go through some quick stretches and a little more warm-up. Ollie moves off each leg perfectly, his movements smooth.

Ryan hasn't ridden a reining pattern since he was nineteen, but still loves the sport. I've been trying to convince him to train one of the colts and enter into the Futurity.

Ollie is our best Reiner, his spins are incredible and his stops are envied throughout the show circuit. We canter our circles, the rush of speed thrilling me. Movement outside the arena catches my eye. Alex, Emma, and Dane join Ryan against the fence as they watch me ride.

The rush of riding a pattern fills me, I love this sport. Moving the reins, I spin Ollie to the right and then the left before finishing off with two sliding stops. The dirt flies on either side of us as we slide. Cheering makes me grin as I walk him around to cool him off.

Patting him on the neck, pride fills me at how effortlessly he completed each task.

Everyone else clears away from the fence, only Alex remaining, his eyes bright with awe. That's the first time he's seen me ride like that. I usually work Ollie early in the morning, before everyone is awake. It's our time together, the time when my thoughts are quiet, rather than running in a million different directions at a speed that would overwhelm most.

When I was a kid, the way my brain functioned was hard to deal with. It didn't take my parents long to realize I needed an outlet, a way to organize the many thoughts going on all at once. They helped me figure out how to sort through everything, focus without getting lost in the noise. Horses are a major factor in allowing me to focus. They draw my attention, making me feel grounded and purposeful. The older I get, the better I am at keeping my brain quiet.

Sliding off, I lead him to the tie stall and remove his tack. A shadow blocks out the light in the barn, warm lips kissing the back of my neck. "Seeing you ride like that, holy shit, is that ever sexy."

Turning in Alex's arms, I suck his lip into my mouth, biting it. Groaning, I lick his lips begging for entrance to his mouth. Alex lifts me, backing me into the stall. My back hits the wall, his hips pushing into mine. Devouring his lips, I want so badly to push him down into the straw.

Being around Alex is like being with the horses. He helps slow down my thoughts, focusing only on what's happening in the moment. He's one of the few people that can do that and he doesn't even know he's having that effect on me. It's one of the reasons I enjoy having him in my life in any capacity I can.

"Hey, Lia . . ." Alex drops me unceremoniously and I move away from him to stand next to Ollie as Dane walks into the barn. "I was wondering if—oh, hey, Alex."

Leaning into Ollie, I hide the smirk as confusion fills his face. It hadn't escaped anyone's notice that Alex and I haven't spent any time together over the past several months, and Dane has been so preoccupied with finishing moving his stuff over to Emma's that he probably thought we were still avoiding each other's company.

"So, Lia, thanks for answering my questions about sliding stops. Maybe when we train up the colt you're picking out for me you can teach me."

He sneaks a wink at me before exiting the barn. Loosening the cinch, I pull the saddle off Ollie's back. "What's up, Dane?" Proud at how casual my voice is, I grin at the suspicious look on his face.

"Oh, yeah. I was hoping I could leave my office in your house. Until Alex finds a place, all the rooms are taken at ours." He leans against the wall, watching me groom Ollie.

Alex is looking for a place? I guess it makes sense, why would he want to live with Emma and Dane, especially once they're married. The idea of not having him close makes my stomach sink.

"Lia?" Dane waves a hand in front of my face, arching his brow at me.

"Yeah, not a problem. I don't need it."

My mind is racing. Where would he move? Since Emma and Dane are getting married, will he still stay here? Or will he move somewhere that isn't quite so isolated?

# CHAPTER FIVE

*Lia*

Gripping Belle's rear right leg, I lean my weight back stretching it as far behind her as she can go. I release her leg after doing some adjustments and grin at the groan she lets loose.

"Feels good, doesn't it, girl?" Cooing at her, I move to her other leg giving it the same attention as the first. An audible pop sounds and she starts licking and chewing, happy with the work I'm doing.

I've already given her a massage, and now I'm finishing up adjusting her so everything is where it should be.

Emma stopped by last night because she'd noticed some tightness when she was riding Belle yesterday, so I woke up early to fit her in before a full day at the clinic. Belle is so expressive and her enjoyment of the treatments is apparent in her responses.

I love my job, helping horses feel better physically, which then changes how they are mentally. Watching horses start out really tight and sore before becoming more relaxed and pain free, it gives me an immense sense of joy and accomplishment. Horses like Belle are simply maintaining a strict routine, others require more intensive treatment due to injuries. I love them all.

Every day I count my blessings to have a job I love. I enjoy my clients, the horses, and the results of my work. Rarely do I have days that I dread. Today is one of those rare, challenging days. And it's all because of one person.

It's not that I haven't seen Lydia around, this community is very small, but it's never close encounters. I'm grateful I don't have either of them in my life anymore, but the sting of betrayal is still there, and I'm not sure how I'm going to react to seeing her. Her horse, Patty, is finally well enough to be trail-ered over here. The vet's work is done, now my job begins.

"Good morning, Lia! How's she doing?" Releasing Belle's leg, I straighten and grin at my best friend. Her cheeks are flushed and she has that in love glow radiating from her.

Part of me twinges in envy, but I remind myself I once did serious and it didn't work out so well for me. Now all I want is no-strings fun. The reaction in my body is instantaneous when I think of all the fun Alex and I have been having over the past couple of weeks, and the envy fades.

"Good morning. She's feeling much better now that I've worked on her a bit. Her hips were out again this morning, they're back in now. I thought we could leave her a couple weeks, but we will need to start treating her weekly again."

"You're awesome." Emma smiles at me, the lighthearted friend from my childhood stands before me and not the shell of a woman who arrived here almost one year ago. "Have you seen that older brother of yours? He was gone when I woke up this morning."

Laughing at her expression of censure at Dane, I shake my

head. "No, but he probably tried to wake you up and wasn't successful. You sleep harder than anyone I know these days."

"That's not a good enough excuse." Laughing, I take Belle's halter off and pat her shoulder affectionately. Resting my hands on my hips, I enjoy a few moments with one of the best people I know.

"How are wedding plans going now that you have a venue?"

"Better. I ordered this wedding planner online and it's been really useful. There is so much to decide on, I'm pretty sure if your parents wouldn't kill him, Dane would be flying us to Vegas for a quick wedding," she laughs, shrugging. "I'm enjoying it, though."

The door to Emma's house shutting draws our attention from chatting while watching Belle trot to the hay stack, we turn to watch Alex bound down the steps. My heart flutters a little at the sight of his messy brown hair.

Carefully controlling my features, I watch passively, trying not to devour the way his hoody hugs his muscles or the perfect fit of his jeans stretching on his muscular thighs. I know every inch of that body, it's spectacular. Part of me wants to lean in to Emma and confess what's going on, but I refrain. I will tell her, sometime, but not right now.

"I'm going to go help Dane and Jesse repair some fences. Samson busted into the pen with the mares." Alex nods a friendly greeting at me and I smile in return. My body responds in a much more reactive way, thoughts of the previous evening playing out like pictures in my head. I love the way his hands feel on my body, the way he can move me easily and the way he challenges me in bed.

"He always did prefer to be with the mares. He thinks he's quite the stud." Licking my lips, I grin as Alex follows the movement before looking away.

Emma laughs. "He really does." She smiles at Alex when he affectionately kisses the top of her head. "Make sure you tell Dane he's in trouble for sneaking out this morning."

"Will do. We will be back in time for breakfast."

Alex walks away and I drop my eyes from his ass to study a scuff on my boot, a smile pulls at my lips when I feel the vibration of my phone. Stuffing my hands into my back pockets, I refrain from checking the message that will surely leave me hot and bothered.

"I'm glad he seems to be over whatever had him acting so weird. In fact, he seems quite jovial these days."

We watch him until he disappears from sight.

Emma audibly sighs after a moment and I look up in concern. "What's wrong, Em?" Climbing the fence, we head over to the house to start cooking, her feet kicking at random rocks causing them to tumble over the driveway.

Our houses look over each other, sharing a driveway. I love that our ranch style home faces her Victorian one. Emma's ten acres are basically enveloped by the vast amounts of land my family owns, kind of how our families always were one close unit.

We bypass her house, heading to my large kitchen where we gather for breakfast daily.

"With Dane living with me full-time now, Alex has been talking about moving. He's even started looking for a place to rent in town. I know that it's only twenty minutes away, it's not like he's moving to Edmonton, but I hate the idea of him not being so close." She leans into the fridge, grabbing all the food we need to make breakfast, before turning back to me and crossing her arms.

"What if he moves in here with me and Ryan?" The question escapes before I can second guess myself, but the excitement that lights up Emma's face is worth it. I try to swallow the accompanying guilt I feel at not sharing my ulterior motives to inviting him to stay here, and ignore the shaking in my hands as the risks of my suggestion run through my mind.

I hate keeping secrets from her, but this whole arrangement is less complicated with no one knowing.

Her grin turns mischievous. "I like the idea of him living here. Close to you. And still close to me. I need my big brother."

"Em, don't get any crazy ideas. You know I don't want anything serious, and from what you've said, neither does Alex."

Pouting, she gives me a playful shove. "Doesn't mean a girl can't dream about her two best friends hooking up."

Grateful my cheeks don't heat with guilt, I pull Emma in for a side hug. "Why don't you spend your days daydreaming about all the disgustingly dirty things you do with my brother? I'm okay, really." Turning on the stove-top, I heat up some olive oil and try to keep my tone light.

"I know you're okay. I never doubt that you are, you're stronger than me, but I know that Graham hurt you. You might be over him, but you're not over what he did." She cocks a perfectly sculpted brow at me, causing me to scowl. "Anyways, even if it's not Alex, I have hope that someone will bust his way into your life and you won't be able to refuse him. Eventually you will find someone who breaks through your reservations and shows you it is okay to trust again." She winks at me, her face breaking out into a look of mischief. "Speaking of dirty things, Dane and I tried this new position last night . . ." She widens her eyes at me and waggles her eyebrows.

"I don't want to know! Gross, that's my brother." Emma laughs and starts prepping the eggs for stuffed French toast.

Despite the amount of work it creates, I've continued to enforce the mandatory breakfast, including Jesse in that rule since he started working here.

Glancing at Emma to make sure she is preoccupied, I pull my phone out of my pocket to check the text message.

> Alex: I've been envisioning you wearing your cowboy boots and hat while riding me, your tight pussy clenching around my cock. Your hands gripping my chest, eyes locked on mine.

Squeezing my thighs together, I swallow hard before finishing reading the message.

> Just as you are about to orgasm, I flip you onto your back and pin your hands above your head, taking away the control you like to fight for. I take you hard and fast until you are biting my shoulder to stop yourself from screaming my name. Your throat raw, voice hoarse from how loudly you shout as you come.

My chest heaves as I struggle to suck in enough air. Sex with Alex is never boring. He is incredibly creative in the bedroom. Smirking at his control comment, I daydream about tying his hands above his head so he can't move. Alex needs the same control I do, he's been betrayed in a different way, but it doesn't diminish the damage to a person's soul.

Something changes inside your heart when the one person you trust the most in the world betrays you. The cut is deeper than most people could ever imagine. Despite the knowledge that not every man will do that, a baser instinct takes over to protect yourself. I often wonder if I will ever be in a place where I can completely succumb, give in and trust my partner to push my limits and take me over the edge I used to crave. Just one more thing Graham stole from me.

I miss the feeling of succumbing. Of being at the mercy of my lover and knowing he will always look after my needs. My overactive brain needs that release. I don't doubt that if I allowed him to, Alex would take care of me. However, I also know that giving in to that instinct, that desire, makes my heart vulnerable to him in a way I feel protected against right now.

Being with Alex is a risk, opening up to him is a risk, because my heart already wants to fall. I can feel it in the way it picks up whenever he's near. I can feel it in the way I not only crave being with him physically, but the way I crave of being with him in every way.

That's why I can't succumb, that surrender means my heart is there for the taking, and he doesn't want it.

Slipping my phone into my back pocket without responding to Alex, I move about the kitchen helping Emma get everything ready. She's distractedly humming to herself, daydreaming about Dane no doubt, and her whisk is no longer moving.

"Em, I think those eggs are ready." Looking over her shoulder, I chuckle as she starts.

She laughs at herself ruefully. "Wow, I zoned out there. Dane was talking in his sleep last night. He was mumbling something about too much tulle." She chews on her cheeks, her lips pulling up into a smile. "I didn't even know he knows what tulle is."

"Hilarious." Chuckling, I hand the freshly sliced bread I

baked yesterday over to her. "So, when did Dane start talking in his sleep? I need dirt that I can bribe him with."

She shakes her head at me, grinning. "I've only heard him talk in his sleep a couple of times, and it's usually only a few words."

"Darn. I've been trying to think of new ways to torture him." Emma just rolls her eyes as she turns on the stove, smiling indulgently. "What? It's my job, as his sister, to be a thorn in his side and I take it very seriously."

We finish preparing breakfast, laughing and chatting about everything that has happened over the past ten months, before moving on to the yearlings and all the different names we've been tossing around. "I still can't believe Ryan named his colt Hoover. That poor horse is going to grow up with a complex."

The door to the kitchen swings open interrupting our giggles and the guys all file in, eyes locked on the food covering the table. Dane beelines over to Emma, wrapping his arms around her and pressing his forehead to hers. They look at each other, silently holding a conversation and the green-eyed monster stirs in my gut once again as I glance at Alex out of the corner of my eye. When I see them together it makes my heart want things my head won't even consider.

*No, this is what I want. No strings, just sex.*

Ryan and Jesse sit in their spots, piling food on their plates, blissfully ignorant to everything going on around them. Alex winks at me and the momentary lapse dissipates as I remember his text, his promise from earlier. It is incredible how one look, one smile from him can calm my doubts. Graham never had that effect on me, there was always some unease hidden deep inside, my gut telling me to be careful.

Dropping into the chair next to Alex, I discreetly run my finger down his thigh before returning my hand to the table top.

"I bet Samson was pretty pissed at being removed from his girls." Chuckling as he grins down at me, I load my plate with a slice of French toast, strawberries, and homemade whipped cream. Breakfast is my favorite meal of the day, and I love to get creative with traditional recipes. I have had stuffed French toast made with cream cheese, but I created my own stuffing from marshmallow whip and Nutella. It's to die for.

"We have a bet going on how many days will pass until he's back in there." Alex reaches under the table, gripping my thigh when I let out a moan as I chew. Leaning in, he whispers, "You better stop making that noise, or our secret won't be a secret anymore."

Swallowing hard, I clench my legs together and resist the temptation to let out another moan.

"So, Alex . . ." Everyone looks over at Emma. "Instead of moving off the property, why don't you move in here? Lia already said it's okay."

I can feel Alex's surprised gaze on my face, reading my reaction. I just turn to him and smile. "There is an empty room."

**Alex**

Sighing with relief as I shut down the website I've finally finished, I remove my glasses, close my eyes and lean my head back onto the couch cushion. Massaging my temples as I will away the pain that has been slowly building. Focusing my mind, I relax the creases in my forehead to help alleviate the ache.

This client has been a pain in my ass, but my headache

stems from the bomb dropped on me at breakfast. Moving in with Lia, that's not string free. That creates a stringy mess, and I don't know how to deal with it.

"You okay?" Emma nudges me with her toe as she looks up from writing. Despite the faraway look in her eyes that she always gets when she is completely focused on a story, she's clearly been paying attention to my suffering.

"Headache. This client has contacted me no less than five times to change her site. I want her to be happy, but good lord! She tells me she wants one thing and then changes her mind after I already made the changes. This time I think I finally have it right." Opening my eyes, I smile at Emma. "How's the book coming?"

My distraction works, her eyes lighting up.

"I actually just finished my rough draft. I've found that things have been flowing a lot more smoothly lately. My rides with Serenity and Belle have been better, I'm being more productive with work, and the nightmares have completely stopped."

"Good. I am so proud of you." Sitting up, I lean forward and kiss the top of her head. "I'm going to take a break. Do you want to go for a ride?" Emma grins at me, her eyes lighting up in excitement.

"Always. I still can't get over how excited I am that you're riding and enjoying it!" Pulling her up from the couch, I laugh as she bounces around the room in excitement.

"I know. I kind of regret my resistance, but with practice and your lessons, I think I'm getting pretty good." I don't mention that Lia has also given me pointers. Somehow my mind always circles back to her. She is everywhere on this ranch, her influence apparent in the way things are built or done.

Chloe bounds into the room, barking playfully as Emma

spins in a circle, whooping about being right. The change in her from when she first moved back here to now still blows my mind. The shadows are gone from under her eyes, she has put on some healthy weight and when she smiles it actually reaches her eyes.

My phone vibrates as we're stepping onto the porch.

> Lia: I'm wearing my cowboy boots and hat, the clinic is empty, and I believe we have some unfinished business.

Hot damn. This woman keeps me on my toes and never ceases to surprise me.

"Ready?" Emma looks at me expectantly. Fuck. How can I ditch my best friend for a booty call? Oh God though, the mental picture of Lia in just her hat and boots has me semi-erect, a fantasy come true.

"I just got a text from a client, I need to deal with this. I'm sorry." The lie falls easily from my lips, something that has never happened with Emma before.

"Okay. Maybe I will saddle up Serenity and go find Dane. Surprise him with a picnic." Emma's eyes light up, relieving me of the guilt I feel for ditching her.

This endeavor isn't supposed to interfere with my life, but I find myself craving more of Lia than I anticipated. Thankfully we're both on the same page and it's working for us, we agreed it wouldn't continue if it started to impact our ability to maintain a friendship if it ended and so far it's been the perfect arrangement.

I step inside the house, and wait for Emma to finish with

Serenity. She takes her sweet ass time, so instead of saddling up Chandler, like I want, I grab one of the ATV's from the shed.

The ride to Lia's clinic seems to take forever, my usual excitement of driving the quad diminished by my need to bury myself in Lia. The trees blur as I speed up, finally seeing the clearing in the distance.

The magnitude of Lia's clinic never fails to take my breath away. Parking the quad, I glance inside the open door to the barn portion. A grin spreads across my face when I remember making use of one of those stalls two days ago. My ass still has a little bit of hay burn.

Stepping into her office, I turn down the hall towards her living quarters. It's a simple layout with a tiny sitting area and kitchen, a small hallway that leads to a bathroom and a small bedroom where she can spend the night when new or severe cases come in. It has proven to be useful in the past couple of weeks. The bed is massive, with a wrought iron bed frame that has come in handy on several occasions.

Taking a deep breath, I barge in the door, skidding to a stop as I look at Lia laying on the bed in her boots, panties, bra and her cowboy hat. Her hazel eyes glimmer with lust as she watches me shut the door, locking it with a resounding click.

I take my time, caressing her with my gaze as I look at every inch of her. She's incredibly beautiful, with her curves, creamy skin, and luscious hair.

Stalking over to her, I groan as she grazes her hand over her hip and up her stomach, her fingers teasing her nipple. Every movement is a taunt.

Pulling my shirt over my head, I growl as she sits up and kneels on the foot of the bed. Lia smirks as she grabs my neck, kissing me fiercely while working the button on my jeans.

"What took you so long?" She grumbles at me as she frees my cock from the confines of my boxer briefs.

"I had to wait for Emma to leave." Sucking her lobe into my mouth, I bite down as she teases the tip of my dick with her thumb.

Sliding my hands down her back, I grumble when she backs away before I can unsnap her bra.

"Uh uh, this is my rodeo." Crouching down, she yanks my pants and boxer briefs down my legs in one swift motion, licking my cock from root to tip as she stands back up.

I've never stuck with a woman who fought me for control before, it's not something I'm willing to give up, but with Lia I can't seem to turn away. The way she battles me is seductive and somehow we both manage to get our needs met.

Lia needs to be in control because she isn't ready to surrender herself to someone. I can see it in her eyes when she pushes me, the battle between what her body craves and what her mind needs. One day she will find someone she can release that need to and surrender herself, I'm not that person and, until then, I have conceded to the fact I have to be lenient if this is going to work.

Lia pushes me down, straddling me. She grinds herself over me, unable to help herself. "Grab the leather straps." Her words are demanding, her eyes showing her vulnerability as she waits for me to fight her.

Ignoring my initial instinct to deny her, I reach above my head and loop the straps over my wrists and hang on, the momentary panic at the inability to use my hands blinding me until I feel her lips wrap around my cock. She never fully ties me, knowing I won't be able to handle it, but my knuckles are white from the strain of forcing my hands to stay put.

The sweet torture of her mouth licking and sucking as she takes me deep down her throat throws every thought in my head away, focusing solely on the way she knows just how to build me up. I hate not being in control, but oh that sweet mouth makes it worth it. The knowledge that she will let me take over settles me as I thrust my hips up.

She takes me into the back of her throat, holding my hips down as she swallows.

"Fuck." I lift my head, watching her lips move over my dick, her eyes on me. "Babe, stop. I'm not coming in your mouth right now."

Lia's face is expressive, her every emotion written clearly for anyone who pays attention. She loves bringing me to the brink, torturing me sweetly until I can't take it anymore. The smirk on her face as she releases me is pure feminine sexuality.

"I've been wet ever since you texted me this morning. The thought of you filling me, taking me hard and fast." She climbs up my body, positioning herself above me before slamming down. "Alex, I want you to fuck me so hard I can't walk straight." She moans my name as she rides me, her nails digging into my chest as she pushes herself up, tightening her muscles as she slams back down, grinding her clit into me.

Resisting the urge to release my hands from their restraint, I watch her ride my dick, her eyes locked on where we join. She throws her head back as she rides me harder until I can't take it anymore.

Letting go of the straps, I grab her hips and flip her onto her back ignoring the disgruntled look on her face as I take back what is mine.

Grabbing her hands, I pin them above her head as I thrust into her, my pace bordering on punishing, just how I have been picturing all day. Her legs wrap around my waist, inviting me in deeper, the new angle enveloping me more firmly. My eyes hold hers as she comes, her pussy gripping my dick as she shudders beneath me. I draw back, pounding back into her as I find my own release.

Pulling out, we get out of bed and start dressing. My eyes linger on her as she covers up her flawless skin.

She smiles at me as she pulls a tank top over her head, and smooths her hair.

Aside from the night we finally gave in, every time we've been together it's like this. Hard, fast, and explosive, usually catching each other in between clients or after everyone has gone to bed for the night, but rarely do we have a chance to linger.

Our first night, I was able to worship her body and I crave the chance to do it again more than I have ever craved being slow with anyone else. I don't do slow, sweet love making, but something about her and the way I feel with her makes me want to slow down. That thought terrifies the shit out of me.

"Umm, so Lydia called yesterday and she's bringing Patty here today. I meant to mention it, but we got distracted." Her eyes are relaxed, despite the prospect of seeing someone who hurt her.

"Okay." Sitting on the foot on the bed, I lean back on my hands and watch her. The concerns from Emma's suggestion this morning returning. "We need to talk about this morning."

Lia's face goes blank, her features carefully schooled to show no emotion. "Okay." She drags the word out.

"I don't know if it's a good idea, it feels serious. I think it's blurring boundaries and I don't want that risk."

"Jesus, Alex. I wasn't suggesting we pick out china patterns. I have a room. You need a room. Not to mention, I was thinking *'hey, easy access.'* We have a bargain, I'm pretty sure the only thing this changes is your location." Lia's expression morphs to one of hurt, and I instantly become defensive.

"It's blurring the lines. Lines that we've established to safeguard ourselves from complicated. Living together would be so far past complicated, I can't even see it behind us."

Lia gets right in my face. "The only fucking reason this has become complicated is because you are making it that way. The bedroom is yours if you want it, if you don't then what the fuck ever. Now get out, I have shit to do without you freaking out on me again over something that's in your damn head."

She leaves me sitting in the bedroom of her clinic, the sheets in a messy pile at the foot of the bed reminding me of how we went from post-orgasmic bliss to angry tension in a matter of minutes. Hanging my head, I silently berate myself. She's right, I'm making a mountain out of a molehill.

She's so pissed off she is willing to face Lydia alone, rather than have me there with her. Shame fills me, Lia has done nothing to make me doubt her commitment to our agreement. In the past two weeks, we've had fun and it's been easy. She texts when she wants me, but otherwise acts no different than she would with Jesse.

I make quick work of tidying up the room, before joining her in her office. Her back is to me, her shoulders hunched forward as she pulls papers from her filing cabinet. I have a feeling she's just avoiding looking at me, and I don't blame her. I can only hope she knows this is about me and not about her.

Stepping in behind her, I push her hair over one shoulder and kiss the side of her neck. She flinches at the contact, making me feel like an even bigger jerk. "I'm an asshole."

She relaxes just a bit, her body curving into mine. "Go on."

"It's easy to forget that you're different from other women who say they're okay with the friends with benefits idea, but mean until it becomes something more." She turns in my arms, smirking up at me.

"Don't be so self-centered. I'm using you for your body, that's it." Her hands run up my chest soothing me. "Haven't we already established that I'm not some clingy chick? We're friends first, fuck buddies second."

Leaning down, I capture her lips with my own, sinking into her as she opens up to me. Before we can take it any further, a car door slams and she pulls away, her eyes suddenly strained.

"What's wrong, baby?" Brushing my fingers down her cheeks, I drop my hand when the door opens, a slender red head walks in. Lia stiffens, the smile on her face tense and guarded.

"Good morning, Lydia." Lia turns to her desk, grabbing a clipboard and pen, before attaching the papers she has stacked on the cabinet. I don't miss the way she has to take a deep breath before turning back around.

Stepping forward, I extend my hand. "Hi, I'm Alex."

Lydia grasps my hand, blatantly checking me out. I drop her hand quickly, narrowing my eyes on the woman who betrayed her friend.

"Sorry, Alex. Lydia is my ex-boyfriend's fiancée. Her horse, Patty, had a nasty fall when they were riding recently and needs some intensive therapy." Lia steps up alongside me, watching Lydia with narrowed eyes.

I wrap my arm around Lia, bending down to kiss her temple. She leans into me, the tension leaving her body.

Looking down, I meet her hazel gaze with a wink, before wrapping my hand around the back of her neck and kissing her fiercely. The need to protect her from this woman hits me like a wall, it's unexpected and confusing.

Pressing my lips to her ear, "Do you want me to stick around, or do you got this?"

She shivers, her hazel eyes burning as she pulls away from me. "I'm okay."

"Okay, I need to go to work. I will see you later, baby." Ignoring Lydia, I leave Lia to do her job, thankful I don't need to stick around after all.

I've never been slammed with the need to protect anyone

before, aside from Emma, but the desire to shield Lia was more primal. I wanted to prove to that hateful woman that Lia is better off without her pathetic friendship and that asshat of an ex. I recognize the jealousy coursing through me when I think of some other man taking her from me. That kind of emotion needs to be locked down.

Once I'm back at the house, I grab my computer and move to join Emma on the couch. My nerves are fried and I need nothing more than to distract myself with work.

She looks up to greet me, bursting into laughter as she takes in my appearance. "Your pants aren't buttoned up. Do I even want to know?"

Looking down, I laugh. "Oops."

"Where have you been? I thought you had work to do?" Emma closes her laptop, shifting her legs to make room for me on the couch.

"I was just four-wheeling around the trails, I dealt with the issue and thought it would be fun to take a break." I could tell her I was hanging out with Lia, but it would lead to more questions than I care to answer. I hate keeping secrets from her, but I like how this is going and I know Emma will pressure me to make it more than it is. Make it more than I'm capable of giving.

"You've been disappearing a lot these days." Emma nudges me in concern with her toe.

"I'm just enjoying country life. Besides, this spring has been incredible, and I want to enjoy it before we get the rain that's in the forecast." She accepts what I'm saying at face value, I've never lied to her before. I've omitted information about my past to save her from the gory details, but never outright lied. It sucks.

We settle in to working, Emma's intense focus helping get me into the zone. I open Dane's website and start making the necessary tweaks. It doesn't take me long to complete the task. Dane and I communicate weekly about updates needed on the website. He's my favorite type of client, he knows what he wants and communicates it with precise notes.

Setting my laptop on the coffee table, I tuck my hands behind my neck and nudge Emma with my foot. "How's Arwen's training coming along?"

"She's fantastic, absolutely amazing." She smiles widely, proud of her little filly. "She's a pro with the halter and being led. That's all I want to focus on right now. Ryan also trimmed her hooves, she stood perfectly. We can start getting her used to tack, so that way when she turns two I can start training her to ride."

We fall silent, Emma's fingers flying over the keyboard as she loses herself to her story. I've never told her, but I've read everything she has written. She specifically told me not to, but I want to support her in any way I can.

I prefer her paranormal stuff to the straight up contemporary, but I actually love her books. I recommend them to clients all the time.

Rolling my head onto the cushion of the couch, I let my eyes drift shut.

*Mom stands in front of the door as I carry my suitcase down the stairs. My back aches from the bruises developing around the cuts from her belt.*

*"You're MY child, not theirs. You can't leave." Her words are slurred, she's already popped some pills and drank a couple of beers, despite the early hour.*

*"You're not a fucking mom. You may be my biological mother, but you quit being my parent the second Dad walked out that door." For the first time in my life, I physically move her away from me. It dawned on me last night as she whipped me with her belt that I'm*

*bigger than her. I refuse to hit her back and sink to her level, but there is nothing she can do to stop me from leaving.*

*"Your dad left because of him." Her hard eyes glare over at Emma's dad, standing on their front lawn with his arms crossed, watching us.*

*"What could Mr. Hayle ever possibly do to drive Dad away from us? You know what, never mind. You're too fucked up to know what you're saying anyways."*

*I'm down the steps, ignoring her as she follows me to the edge of the lawn. Crying, begging, pleading. I can see Emma watching from the window of her house, her face white. I give my head a shake, continuing on my path without looking back. I'm taking control of my life, and I will never lose it again.*

I wake with a start when my foot falls off the couch, the memory of the day that changed my life causing my heart to pound. Glancing up, I watch Emma work. She's still intensely focused, her eyes glued to her screen as I stand and stretch. She will never truly understand what she and her family did for me. Most of the physical scars have faded, but the emotional ones will always be there.

I need to move, the thundering rush in my ears as I try to lock away those memories where they belong. Leaving the living room, I almost knock Lia to the ground as I round the corner into the hallway.

She pushes me into the wall, wrapping a leg around my waist as she presses hard kisses onto my neck, before leading me upstairs.

Shutting my bedroom door, she shoves me against it, her lips hard against mine as her hands run up and down my body. She grabs the bottom of my t-shirt, lifting it over my head before kneeling to remove my pants.

Fisting my hands at my sides, I let her have the control, banging my head against the door when her lips wrap around my cock. She sucks hard, before taking me all the way to the back of her throat, swallowing.

My hands fist in her hair, my hips moving as I push her head where I want her, growling as she sucks my dick. She fights my hands, running her tongue up to the tip, teasing the head.

Yanking her off me, she pushes me onto the bed, fighting me to regain the power. Lia straddles me, kissing me forcefully as she lowers herself onto my dick, clenching around me. My arms are pinned above my head, her small hands wrapped around my wrists and I hate that I love it so much. The anxiety is there, the loss of control making my heart race, especially after the dream I had less than twenty minutes ago, but seeing her wild and in control helps drown it out.

Part of me recalls the easy going kid I used to be, but after the abuse I went through with my mom, I can't handle feeling out of control. It takes me back to her drugged and drunken outbursts, when she would burn me with cigarettes or lock me in the basement without dinner.

Lia takes away the anxiety I feel at succumbing, even if I prefer to control her. There is something so sexy seeing her give in to me.

Flipping Lia onto her back, I pin her arms the way she had mine and fuck her, covering her mouth as she cries out, her pussy clenching around me like a vice. My body quakes with the power of my release, sweat beading at the back of my neck.

Planting a kiss on her lips, I leave her to go clean up before crawling back into bed. Instead of getting up and dressing like usual, she lays on her side to face me. "Thanks for being there when she arrived today. It helped me get through the initial appointment. I can't believe I was best friends with someone like her. I just like to give people the benefit of the doubt, but

Dane and Ryan never liked her, and their gut instinct with people tends to be quite good."

Grinding my teeth, I breathe deeply. The thought of someone doing that to Lia pisses me off. She's so fucking amazing, what kind of fool would let her go. *Like you're going to?*

"They don't deserve your energy, you're too great of a person to spend any amount of time thinking about them." Brushing some hair off her forehead, I search her eyes to see if she believes me.

"I know. It's been almost three years, and I'm honestly over it." She sits up, the sheet pooling around her waist leaving her perfect breasts bare. "I've realized that I'm happier now than I ever was with Graham. There was always something lacking from our relationship."

Smiling, her eyes shine as she kisses me deeply before crawling out of bed and dressing. Standing, I pull my jeans on, making sure to do up the button. Lia is about to open the door when there is a knock. She turns to me, eyes wide, before bolting into my bathroom.

Opening the door, I smile at Emma. "What's up?"

She looks at me oddly, probably wondering why I'm shirtless and looking like I just got out of bed. I can't stop the grin that forms when her forehead creases as she peers into my room. "You're acting weird."

"I was just busy."

Shaking her head, she leans on the doorframe, wisely choosing not to ask what I was doing. "Anyways, whatever you have going on tomorrow evening clear it. We're all going to Linger."

"I have no plans."

"Good." She looks behind me again, her brows pinched together, before going into her room and shutting the door.

Lia comes out of the bathroom, her hand covering her mouth to muffle her laugh. "I need to go. See you tomorrow morning."

She brushes past me, her fingers trailing across my abs. I lean against the frame, listening as she rushes down the stairs, backing into my room when I hear the front door shut.

# CHAPTER SIX

*Alex*

Ryan and Jesse wave as we enter Linger, our favorite bar and a secret treasure. The exterior looks like it should be condemned, but the inside is warm and inviting. The chandelier in the middle of the room is the central focus. It was hand blown by a local glassblower, and I would love to take a trip to his shop one of these days.

Lia steps up next to me, drawing my eyes down to her. She looks absolutely stunning, her dress fits perfectly to her body. When she walked onto the porch this evening, it was all I could do not to touch her and kiss her.

Even now, I want to wrap my arm around her, show off that she is mine. A feeling I have no right to. She steps in front of me, her hips swaying as she walks. The low lighting in Linger is romantic, heightening my already intense attraction to her, especially with the way her eyes shine as we move to join our friends.

Seeing Emma and Dane together on a daily basis is messing with me. It's making me want something like that, wishing I was capable of believing that they were the norm and not the exception, but then I remember my scumbag father and my substance abusing mother. Growing up watching their dysfunctional marriage made me hate the idea. At one time they were happy. I remember them going out on dates, both of them smiling as they dressed up. As I got older, I started seeing through the facade.

Besides, after experiencing the ultimate betrayal from my parents, neglecting to fulfill their most basic duty, my trust isn't easily given. Mostly, though, I don't trust myself. I don't trust myself to completely open up to anyone, and I know that will be the ruin of any relationship I go into.

Trusting Lia with what we have is already a stretch. I've never spent so much time with a lover before. She makes everything easy, and that frightens me because losing sight of our boundaries is something I foresee happening with her.

Sliding into the booth next to Lia, I order a beer from the waitress who is hovering near our table. She's eyeing up Ryan and by the way he's looking back, I'm positive she won't be going home alone tonight.

"Where's Ashton?" Lia leans forward to ask Jesse, shouting over the music.

"He's on a date." Jesse tips his beer back, watching the crowd in the bar. It's no secret that Jesse is attracted to his roommate, despite his frequent denials. The disappointment is written on his face and I feel bad for him. Attraction is hard enough without adding in being attracted to the person you live with. Not to mention how unsupportive his father is. He hasn't spoken to him since coming out last summer.

Dane and Jesse start talking about the ranch, causing Emma to roll her eyes. "No. We're not working tonight. In fact, let's go dance until you have to carry me out of here." Dane smiles at her and leads her to the dance floor.

Lia leans onto Jesse's shoulder, watching the dancers. I can see the envy in her eyes. I don't want her to regret what we have, so I yank her out of the booth to dance. When she looks at me, a question in her eyes, I simply shrug. "Friends can dance, can't they?"

"Oh, definitely." Her smile is bright, but it doesn't quite reach her eyes. My chest constricts, it's rare that Lia lets things get her down and I wonder what's running through her head. Holding her close on the dance floor, the fruity scent of her shampoo intoxicates me.

The song ends, many of the dancers heading to the bar to get another drink. I tighten my arms when I feel her start to pull away. "Let's dance a while longer."

She relaxes, two-stepping with me to the country song the DJ is playing.

Every time the song ends, I refuse to let go until she quits trying to pull away.

"Are you okay?" After four songs, I can't hold it in any longer. Her eyes still lack the happiness that usually makes them shine and it bothers me.

"Yeah, I just have a lot on my mind." She smiles brightly, her eyes clearing a little. "All of Dane's stuff is out of his room, if you've decided to take it."

Understanding dawns, we never really came to a decision on me moving in, and I can see that she is worried about me overreacting again.

"I started packing today."

The smile that lights her eyes makes all my doubts fly away. Everything up to this point has worked. Besides, I see her all the time anyway, so living across the hall won't change things that much. Thinking about it that way makes it easy to justify. When this friends-with-benefits whatever ends and she moves on, I can always continue to search for an apartment.

Emma and Dane dance by, completely enraptured in each other. Lia's arms wrap more firmly around me, her head resting on my chest as a slow song starts. We're swaying on the crowded dance floor when her body tenses briefly. Following where she is looking, I see Lydia walk in with some guy.

Realizing that must be Graham, I feel my body fire with anger. He's not even a real man. A real man would tell the woman he is with that he wants to move on. He wouldn't give her a key to his place and start banging her best friend shortly after. Some best friend. I may not always be up front with Emma, mostly to shield her, but I would never betray her.

Grasping Lia's hand, I lead her to an open spot at the bar, walking past where they are standing. Lia gapes up at me, unsure how to respond to the fierce look on my face. I don't know what I'm doing, but I want to claim her in front of him.

Lydia is watching us, and it doesn't take her long to drag Graham over.

"Hey, Lia." Lydia's smile is friendly, wavering when Lia remains stoic. She presses on. "How's Patty doing?"

"She's coming along. It will be a couple of weeks before we notice a significant difference." Lia leans into me for support as she finally looks at Graham. He hasn't taken his eyes off her. I want to kick him in his nuts. "Graham, Alex. Alex, this is Graham."

"Her boyfriend." I clarify, holding my hand out.

He stiffly shakes my hand, wincing at my hard grip, before he pulls away and stands there uncomfortably as Lydia tries to talk to Lia.

Lowering my head, I kiss Lia's neck, her body automatically

relaxing into me. I can feel her pulse pounding and I smile knowing it's from what I'm doing to her neck and not being near Graham. I didn't doubt Lia when she said she was over the whole thing, but I needed to show him what he lost. He doesn't need to know what his betrayal did to her ability to trust.

I don't doubt that the day will come that she will entrust someone with her heart again. She has too much passion and too big of a heart not to find someone to share it with.

"I think we're going to head back to the dance floor now." Leading her away, I hold her close as we dance. Her eyes never venturing in their direction again.

"I would apologize, but I'm not sorry." Murmuring into her ear, I grin as she shivers and presses herself into me.

"I'm not sorry either. I haven't seen him in years and I admit I was shocked watching them walk in, but after it wore off I felt nothing." This time when she smiles at me, the smile reaches her eyes.

Countless songs later, we rejoin our group at the table.

"Did I see you kiss my sister?" Dane looks between us, Emma smirking beside him. Crap, I didn't think about the repercussions on my actions. I'm not ready for anyone to know about what's happening, especially since I don't think her brothers will appreciate the fact we're having casual sex. Swallowing hard, I'm saved from having to answer.

"We ran into Lydia and Graham. I asked him to act as my boyfriend because I thought it would help. It's silly, I know." Lia smiles at me in fake apology.

"You haven't seen them together since shortly after the break up. Are you okay?" Emma looks at Lia in concern.

"I'm fine. I'm over it."

Emma grins as Lia states this, her eyes glancing at me quickly before turning away. Rolling my eyes, I don't bother saying anything. Now that she has Dane, it's only a matter of time before she starts in on me.

"Finally. That asshole didn't deserve any of your attention." Dane glares daggers over to the bar. My lips lift in a smirk as I see Graham and Lydia glance over here and cringe.

"Dane, stop it. Seriously, it's fine." Lia slides out of the booth, shooting a warning look at Dane. "I'm going to the bathroom, leave them alone. It's been almost three years."

Watching as she makes her way to the bathroom, I narrow my eyes when I see Lydia push Graham in that direction. Emma, Dane, and Jesse are huddled together chatting. Ryan has disappeared somewhere, probably flirting with the waitress, so I slip out of the booth and follow them.

The bathrooms are at the end of a long, dark hallway. I can hear Lia's voice as I approach. "What do you want, Graham?"

Her voice shows no emotion aside from exasperation. Leaning against the wall, I wait and listen. It's rude and I should probably just go back to the table, but I want to make sure she's okay.

"I know it's been a long time and I know by now it probably doesn't matter, but I want to apologize." His words sound stilted, like he's rehearsed this, but never gotten comfortable with the words. "Not that I showed it at the end, but I did care about you and you deserved so much more than that."

Lia sighs and I can imagine the expression on her face. He sounds sincere, despite the strain in his voice and I'm positive she will forgive him. That's just who she is. "Okay. I just have one question. You both knew me better than that. I would have let you go without hesitation had you talked to me."

"I know. Neither of us are proud of how we got started."

"Well, if it makes any difference, I forgive you. I think I forgave you a long time ago." Backing away, I leave them to finish their conversation.

I know that she said she got closure before, but now that he's apologized, I know that now she really has the closure she needed.

A lead weight sinks in my stomach as I realize that means she might finally be in a place where she is ready to open herself up again, there will be nothing holding her back from letting me go for someone who can provide her with something meaningful, something more than incredible sex.

I'm not ready to let her go. That point in time seems like it's further in the distance than I ever anticipated.

# CHAPTER SEVEN

*Lia*

"Hyatt Equine Therapy, Lia speaking, how may I help you?" Bracing the phone between my ear and shoulder, I save the treatment plan I've been working on for a new client. I currently have five horses on the premises, and two new ones coming two days from now.

"Hi, Miss Hyatt, this is Georgiana Waters from Parkland University. I'm one of the on-campus counselors." Leaning back in my chair, I tuck a strand of hair behind my ear as I listen to the woman on the other end of the line spiel on about her role at the university thirty minutes away. "I'm calling because I have an odd request for you."

"I'm not sure how I can help you, your University doesn't have an Equine Therapy program." Grabbing a pen, I start doodling on the notepad in front of me, sure that she called me by mistake somehow.

"I'm not calling with regards to our programs, I'm actually

calling in regards to a particular student who has recently started coming to see me once a week. I can't go into details for confidentiality reasons, but traditional therapy isn't doing anything for her. I thought based off your website that we might be able to work out an arrangement with you."

I open my mouth to protest. I'm not trained to provide therapy for someone.

"Before you say anything, what I was thinking isn't traditional therapy. I thought perhaps you could use some help at the clinic, and it would give her a chance to have an outlet for what she's going through. Animals don't expect you to talk or share, they just expect kindness, and I think this would be good for her." Ms. Waters finishes in a rush, and my heart aches for the girl who has obviously earned a special spot in this woman's heart.

I would have to train her, and if she's never been around horses I would need to incorporate horsemanship lessons into the days she comes to work, but something in my gut says to do this. I have a feeling that this could lead somewhere great, and I've been contemplating taking on an apprentice. If she does well, and enjoys it, maybe she would want to fill that role.

"I have two new horses coming in two days, I'm assuming she's off for the summer so if this is something that interests her tell her to be here at ten in the morning." I rattle off my email, asking her to provide it to the girl, waving off her thanks before disconnecting the call.

Staring at my phone, I feel excited at the idea of giving someone this opportunity. I know how healing horses can be, and she may never open up to me, but hopefully she will find what she's searching for.

Opening my laptop, I search for my disclaimer document and start putting together a packet for her. Damn . . . I should have gotten her name.

I'm so involved in arranging the file, I don't notice Alex until he's sitting on the edge of my desk. "That's one intense look you have going on there."

Looking up at him, I can't fight the smile that automatically stretches across my face. "I had the most bizarre phone call not even five minutes ago."

I grab the papers from my printer, stapling them and putting them in the appropriate spots in the new file I've built as I fill Alex in on the call from Ms. Waters.

"Wow. I'm proud of you." He leans down to press a gentle kiss to my lips. "That's quite the compliment. She must have heard about you from someone and then went looking for your website."

Flushing at his praise, I lean back in my chair devouring him with my eyes. Alex is in his typical attire of jeans and a t-shirt, his hair messy from his hands running through it, and I chuckle when I see his glasses are sitting on top of his head. "Thanks."

"Are you done for the day?" He takes my hand in his, sliding his thumb over my knuckles, sending sparks up my arm.

It's only been a few days since we danced and kissed at Linger, and I've been avoiding him. Mostly I've been avoiding my reaction to being near him since I felt what it would be like to be his, even for a short time.

It's been easy, keeping busy with things that need to be done, allowing him space to move into Dane's empty room. Tonight will be his first official night and my body is tied in knots.

Ever since that night, something shifted and I've been processing how to deal with it. I realized that I want more from a relationship than just sex, but I also realized I want it with Alex, putting me in a complicated spot. That realization hasn't been easy to come to terms with.

Glancing at the time, I see that it's past dinner time, my stomach growling at the realization. "Yeah. I didn't realize how late it had gotten."

"You've been working a ton these past few days." He cocks his head to the side, watching me. I carefully school my features to safeguard the inner turmoil I've been facing. I'm not giving him up, so I need to control these new urges.

"I know, I thought you might like some space to pack. Are you all settled in now?" Shutting down my computer, I shove my chair in and round my desk. Alex wraps his hands around my waist, pulling me into him.

"Yep. I'm unpacked and everything is put away. Dane is going to move his office over this week, I was hoping to set up some space in the room once he's done, if that's okay."

Nodding, I lean my forehead onto his shoulder, breathing in his soft cologne. "I don't need it."

The idea of him moving into more than just one room makes me happy, part of me becoming exactly the girl he is worried I will become.

"You okay?" His voice is concerned and I need to distract him from delving too much into the chaotic thoughts running around my head.

Tilting my head up, I kiss him hard, biting his lower lip before sucking it into my mouth. "Need you."

He picks me up, wrapping my legs around his waist, and walks us into the living quarters of my clinic.

Rousing from a deep night's sleep, I freeze, something feels different. My blankets are wrapped around me tightly, I'm trapped, and my heart starts racing in the warm cocoon. I hate feeling stuck, like I can't escape. When I try to move, a groan rumbles in my ear and the pressure is released with a jolt of awareness.

Eyes springing open, I roll my head over and see Alex next to me, one arm underneath my back and the other now flung across the bed. My brain wakes up with an abruptness as I recall never leaving my clinic.

Shit. We've never spent the night together, always sleeping in our separate beds. My heart aches to curl into him and go back to sleep, but my head knows I need some distance to process this. Rolling out of bed, careful not to wake Alex, I dress quickly and sneak out the door.

Releasing the breath I've been holding once I'm outside my clinic, I laugh as I do the walk of shame to my house. My hair is sticking up all over the place, my makeup smudged underneath my eyes. I'm the poster girl for a one-night stand, even though we've had many nights.

The walk isn't long, though I usually choose to ride to my clinic, and soon I'm breaking through the trees into the yard.

Wheels crunch as Ryan's car pulls into view. Groaning as he waves, I scramble to think of a reason for me to be walking around this hour looking like I do. It's futile, though, so I wait for him to park, resigned to the fact my secret is no longer a secret. There is only one person on this property that would make me look like this and Ryan won't have trouble putting two and two together.

When he gets out of his car, we eye each other up before laughing. We both have the same rumpled and sexed up look. "Someone had a good night."

"I could say the same for you." He smirks at me. "Alex, huh? I kind of thought something was going on. Why all the sneaking around?"

There is no judgement in his tone. Ryan is an amazing big

brother and incredibly protective of us all, but one of his biggest character flaws is that he is a bit of a man whore.

Sitting on the front step to our house, I shove my hair away from my face. "We're not in a relationship, we're just messing around. It's easier to hide it so there is no pressure to be more than what we are."

Ryan knows my hang-ups on giving my heart to someone new, but by the look in his eyes I know he sees through my flippant comment.

"As long as you know what you're doing." He bumps me with his hip, his smile gentle.

"Alex isn't in a place to commit to someone and when I finally do give my heart away, I want the person to be ready to accept it. At the same time, he's someone safe. When we're together it's effortless, easy. We have fun and we don't argue about silly things. I'm okay." I don't know if I'm reassuring him or myself, but we both know that at some point I won't be okay with this anymore. This is why I haven't been with anyone since Graham, it's too easy for my heart to get involved. It's already grasping at the what-ifs.

What if he changes his mind?

What if he just needs a push?

"I get it. I won't say anything to anyone." He wraps his arm around my shoulder, wrapping me in his protective bubble. "Just be careful. You're a sweet person, I don't want to see you get hurt."

"We have ground rules set up. If we feel it's interfering with our ability to maintain a friendship, we will end it. That's the main one, but we also promised it wouldn't interrupt our life or other relationships. So far, it's been going really well." Smiling at Ryan, I squeeze him into a hug. I'm so lucky to have brothers I can talk to about anything. Not that I would share the naughty details, but for him to be so understanding is incredible. They've always let me pave my own path.

Ryan ruffles my hair. "Okay, I'm going to go shower. Hey, can you make blueberry pancakes this morning? I've been craving them."

"You got it."

Changing out of yesterday's clothes, I toss a load of laundry into the wash before mixing up the batter for blueberry pancakes. It felt really weird to wake up next to Alex. I haven't woken up in another man's bed since Graham.

I used to love the feeling of being wrapped up in Graham's arms. The security and warmth of being close to someone was an incomparable feeling. However, after years of sleeping independently, I am not big on cuddling anymore. When Emma and I have sleepovers, I stay on my side of the bed. Even this morning, I was rigidly on the left half of the bed, he's the one that had gravitated towards me, invading my space.

Yet the urge was there. The urge to turn into him, allowing his strength to envelop me in the cocoon his presence creates.

Tossing handfuls of blueberries into the pancake batter, I mix it all together and it's ready to pour onto the skillet by the time Emma strolls into the kitchen. "Good morning." Her voice is hoarse, her hair pulled up into a messy pony tail. She beelines it for the coffee pot, pouring a mug and handing it to me before serving herself. She groans as she sits at the island, cupping the mug of coffee tightly in her hands.

"What's up, buttercup?" Pulling out a chair next to her, I eye her in concern.

"I didn't sleep well and we overslept, making Dane crabby. As if one crabby man wasn't enough, Alex woke up on the wrong side of the bed too." She grimaces as she drinks her coffee, too tired to care that her tongue is getting burned. "I don't even know why he was at our house this morning; he's supposed to be living here now."

Setting my untouched mug down, I start the burner and set about cooking the pancakes, trying to decipher why Alex would be in a bad mood. Dread fills me when I wonder if it's because we spent the night. If anything is going to set him off, it's the blurring of boundaries.

The guys start crowding into the kitchen, all except Alex. They're chattering loudly, but Emma and I exchange a look when Dane informs us that he ran into Alex outside and he's skipping breakfast today.

Everyone waits for me to make a big deal out of it, for anyone else I would, but I shrug indifferently knowing that it's not my place to force him to eat here.

Setting the platter hosting a mountain of pancakes onto the table, I shove aside the uneasy feeling that I might have caused this and jump into the conversation with my usual enthusiasm. By the time we've finished breakfast I've convinced myself it couldn't possibly have to do with me.

After everyone leaves and the kitchen is clean, I head up to my room. My day is clear and Emma has been keeping me stocked in book recommendations. Curling up on my window seat, the sun beaming in providing a cozy heat. Powering up my device, I start a series Emma had raved about.

It doesn't take long for me to lose myself in the story. This is what I need, an escape. When I read, my mind loses itself in the story, but I usually come out of it knowing the answers to questions I'm struggling with. It's almost as though focusing on an entirely different world frees up the space in my head to make decisions I waver on.

I don't put my book down, ignoring everything until the light has dimmed so much that I have to flip on my lamp.

Clasping the reader to my chest, I sigh happily. How Emma knows exactly the type of book I need always surprises me.

This story is funny, romantic, and quirky.

"Do I even want to ask what that look is for?" Ryan leans in my doorway, grinning at the dreamy expression on my face.

"Emma recommended a book to me and it's making me swoon. What's up?" Uncurling my legs, I stand and walk over to Ryan, pushing him out the door. He follows me down the stairs and into the kitchen, chuckling.

"Nothing, I was just passing by and saw you smiling like a goof." He grabs a couple of glasses from the cupboard and pours us some wine. "Have you heard from Alex at all today? I haven't seen him around the house."

The reminder that Alex didn't show up for breakfast and has now gone the longest span of time in a while without texting takes away the satisfied feeling of reading a good book.

"No, but we don't really text aside from—well, you know." Shrugging, I smirk at the grossed out look on his face.

"I'm not one to talk when it comes to no-strings attached sex, but I have to admit it feels weird knowing your sister is doing that." He gives me a half grimace, half grin and I burst out in laughter.

Ryan leans against the counter, women find him very attractive and I wonder if anyone will ever be able to snag him. He would make an amazing husband and father. I don't even know why he won't commit. Dane was committed to Emma from childhood. I tried it and was hurt. Ryan has always liked to play the field.

We chat for a while, polishing off the bottle of wine. Scouring the kitchen, I fix up supper for Ryan and me, setting aside some for Alex in case he decides to come home from wherever he is. My head is fuzzy from the wine and skipping lunch, making it difficult for me to control my thoughts.

Shortly after we eat, Ryan takes off and I know he's meeting some woman.

Checking my phone hopefully, I'm filled with disappointment that Alex still hasn't texted me or come home.

Biting my lip, I wonder if I should just give us a day off. I need to get my head on straight anyways, and finishing this love story will hopefully give me the dose of happily ever after I need, allowing me to continue on like normal tomorrow.

~

**Alex**

Shutting down my computer, I rummage through my bedside table to find some aspirin. I've been locked in my room all day, working until my eyes are crossed.

When I awoke alone in Lia's clinic this morning I was shocked to discover it pissed me off, which is completely ridiculous and I don't even want to delve into the why's of that.

Then, to top it off, that damn client called to make changes to the website I'm designing for her, again. Usually I don't care about making changes, but it's never small changes with this woman, it's completely revamping the entire website. We haven't even published it yet and she's done five complete changes. I ignored her website today because I didn't have the patience to work on it.

Crawling out of bed, I dig through the clutter on my floor and try to find my phone. About halfway through the day I had chucked it off the bed to resist texting Lia. Given my reaction to waking alone, I thought some distance would be a good idea, but all it's done is put me in a bad mood.

Finally finding it, I check my screen. A couple texts from Emma and one from my mother. As usual, seeing her name just fills me with anger. I never respond, but I allow her to text so I know she is still alive.

Pocketing my phone, I crash back onto my bed trying to compartmentalize my thoughts. I feel scattered and I know without a doubt it's because of the woman across the hall.

Maybe it's a good thing she wasn't in my bed this morning, it would have felt too intimate. I'm not supposed to want to wake up next to her, clearly the lines of friendship and sex are blurring. We need to keep it defined and clear cut, so there are no risks of getting hurt because I know I will end up hurting her if this goes too far. It's inevitable.

A soft knock at my door followed by Emma's head popping into my room makes me smile. She is the most important person in my life. My savior. She doesn't even have a clue, just a basic understanding of what I went through. People come and go, but our friendship is everlasting and the only constant in my life.

I don't have faith in people and their ability to work through tough situations. Emma is different, there is a deep connection I feel with her that I've never felt before. People talk about soulmates, Emma is the friend version of that. She came into my life exactly when I needed her the most and has never left.

"Hey, Em." Patting the bed next to me, I roll onto my side as she sits down, legs folded underneath her. "Why aren't you at home?"

"You've been holed up in here all day. I know you snuck past us while we were eating this morning. Talk to me. What's going on?" Her bright green eyes are knowing, making me almost blurt out that I'm screwing her best friend for sport. Almost.

"It's just one of those days. I didn't feel capable of dealing with anything but the mess in my head." She holds out her hand, waiting for me to grab it and we sit silently just like we had when we were teenagers.

She never presses me for more than I can give, which is why she is the only person in this world that I trust. When her parents died, it felt like I lost my own family. As a kid, I thought I saw a resemblance in myself to her father. It was wishful thinking that I didn't come from a family as fucked up as mine.

My father started a new family while with my mother, never connecting with me. I remember as a young child he used to have time for me, it diminished around the time Emma moved in until he left a few years later.

My mother was an enigma. I faintly recall a doting parent. Someone to play with me and cuddle with me. Something happened when I was school-aged with her and Dad, she withdrew from us, gradually turning to substances. I suspect she always had a problem, but it was under control until Dad left.

*Mom staggers into the room, her pupils are so large, I can't even see any hazel. She looks kind of possessed.*

*"Ah. There you are. The light of my life, my very reason for living." Sarcasm drips from her voice. She moves towards me, unsteady, until her hand lands on my shoulder, gripping so hard I know there will be fingerprints. "Where's your little friend today?"*

*My heart pounds. Emma and her family went camping for the weekend, they invited me but Mom said no, not that she remembers. "Camping." I bite out.*

*"Pity." Her eyes turn cold as her grip tightens and she steers me to the basement. I could fight her, but I can't bring myself to, so I let her push me around. I know what's coming, so I'm prepared for the push as she shoves me down the stairs, slamming the door shut and*

*locking it. Who knows how long I will be down here until she remembers to let me out.*

"You know, you never have to bear the burden of whatever's bothering you alone. Never give up hope that there will be someone who makes you forget the weight on your shoulders. Someone who will help you leave it in the past." She squeezes my hand, not letting go as she lies on her side facing me.

"What if I don't want to forget? They say when you forget the past you're destined to repeat it." I can't help but laugh when she rolls her eyes.

"Don't even start." She sits back up, getting off my bed and pulling me with her. "You haven't eaten hardly anything at all today. Let's go raid Lia's fridge."

My stomach growls loudly in response as I follow her to the kitchen. On the island sits a Tupperware container with a post-it note on top with my name.

"I guess Lia already thought of you." Ignoring the tone in Emma's voice, I pop the lid. My mouth waters at the still hot chicken alfredo.

"Mom texted me today." Her eyes widen at my revelation, watching me as I devour the pasta.

"Seriously? It's been . . . what? Nine months?" She hops onto the stool next to me, completely stunned.

"Yeah, that sounds about right." Scratching the back of my head, I have to admit, despite the hatred I feel towards my mother, I was worried.

"What did it say?" Wordlessly, I pull up the text I haven't read yet.

"Alex. I went by your apartment and a stranger was there. Why didn't you tell me you moved? I went to tell you I've been sober for a month and I want to see you." I read out loud, emotionless.

She knows I refuse to see her if she's under the influence of anything, but I no longer get excited when she tells me she's been sober for one month. She's done that before, but without any real help she always relapses.

Shutting my phone off, I can feel Emma's warring emotions. She has no love for my mother, and before her parents passed away she would have been ranting and raving about how she has lost any right to see me. However, she knows that time is precious and limited, so sometimes she wavers and thinks I should reach out to at least one of my parents.

"Are you going to reply?"

"Probably not. I know part of you doesn't agree with that decision, but I have the only family I need sitting right here." Standing, I put my dirty dishes in the dishwasher. Her arms wrap around me from behind in a quick squeeze before I walk her to the front door.

Once she's gone, I head back upstairs, pausing outside Lia's door. The light is on in her room, but instead of knocking, I turn and walk into my bedroom, shutting the door behind me.

I'm ready for this day to be over. Tomorrow will go back to normal. I will go see Lia at the clinic and put this mood behind me. I spent too many years feeling unwelcome and miserable in my parents' house, I refuse to be that way here.

# CHAPTER EIGHT

*Alex*

I jolt upright in bed, my heart pounding in my chest with a fear I haven't felt in years. Hands had been grabbing mine, and it brought back terrible memories of my mother dragging me out of bed in a rage.

My eyes search the room before they lock on Lia, sitting on my bed, back pressed against the wall. Her eyes are wide as she watches me, her chest rising and falling rapidly.

"Shit, Lia. I'm sorry." Running my fingers through my hair, I collapse back onto my pillow. She swallows, before crawling over to me and lying next to me, still not touching me.

"No, I'm sorry. I wanted to try and wake you up in a fun, sexy way. I forgot Emma mentioned you don't deal well with being surprised out of sleep." She inches closer, watching me the entire time, before resting her chin on my chest, her eyes remorseful. "I'm sorry I ran off yesterday morning. I haven't slept next to anyone in a long time, and I panicked a little."

Smirking, I hold my fingers close together. "Just a little. If I'm being honest, I might have reacted that way too if I had been the one to wake up first."

"I spent a lot of time thinking yesterday. I think we're over-analyzing all of our actions. Let's just do what feels right. We know what will work for us." She presses her lips onto my chest, her eyes heating as she licks and kisses her way down my stomach.

She whispers something before biting my hip bone, it sounded like *I missed you,* but before I have time to think about it her mouth is wrapped around my cock. I lose myself in the feeling of her licking and sucking until I can't take it anymore.

Yanking her up my body, I flip her onto her stomach and pin her arms above her head. Instead of fighting me like she usually does, she moans and presses her luscious ass into me. Leaning down, I press kisses along her shoulders and in the crook of her neck.

"Do not move your hands." Releasing my grip, I kiss my way down her spine before biting each of her ass cheeks. She moans and spreads her legs, her pussy is glistening with how wet she is.

Part of me wonders if I should be worried at how easily she is giving me the control, but I realize that I missed seeing her yesterday and I don't want to think about anything else. Running my hands down her back, I watch the way her body responds to me. It's erotic to watch her skin respond to my touch, to see how aroused she gets by just my hands.

Leaning down, I lick her pussy until her body is shaking with need. Pulling back, I hold her hips and slam into her.

"God, yes." Lia's moan is guttural, her hands fisting my sheets as I move. "Faster."

Grinning at the command, I slow down, groaning as she clenches around me and growls. She lowers her chest to the bed, changing the angle and I can't hold back anymore. I thrust into her, my eyes glued to where we join. She shivers as her body clenches around mine, her orgasm ripping through her as she cries out my name.

I need to see her.

Pulling out, I flip her onto her back before driving back into her. Her hips lift as she meets me thrust for thrust, our eyes locked together as I come. Dropping to my elbows, I press my forehead to hers.

"If anyone is in the house, they definitely heard us." Lia laughs at my comment, her warm breath teasing my collarbone.

"Good thing I snuck in here after Ryan left for the barn." She starts tracing soft circles on my stomach, smiling to herself as she chews on her lip.

Running my thumb over it, I tilt her chin back up to look at me. "What's on your mind?"

Her eyes drop away, this is the first time I've ever seen Lia shy, and it makes my curiosity flare. "Ummm, I have a surprise for you after breakfast."

Arching my brow at her, I chuckle when she glares at it before sitting up in bed. She hops up and starts dressing, grumbling about eyebrows and how she needs to cook breakfast.

*Lia*

Breakfast was quick this morning, Dane and Jesse rushing out to repair some broken fences as soon as they were done eating.

Emma and Ryan are laughing at the table, high off of the pot of coffee they've both inhaled.

Alex starts clearing the table, moving to sit when the kitchen is spotless. Standing, I push Alex out the door, ignoring the two sets of eyes watching us. I'm too excited to show him the surprise to care. Besides, Ryan already knows, and I can deal with Emma.

"In a hurry?" Alex laughs as I maneuver him through the house, tapping my foot impatiently as he puts his shoes on.

I would be lying if I said I wasn't anxious about this. He had mentioned wanting a colt and asked me to find the perfect one, so I picked one out for him. I can't wait to see him and his horse bond. In a few years I can train it for him, and possibly even teach Alex how to rein.

My heart stutters. *A few years? Shit.*

I'm not supposed to be thinking in the future with Alex, but somewhere along the way, our friends with benefits arrangement has started to transform into more.

When did that happen?

*No. Lia, you can fucking do this. I swear, don't fuck this up because you can't control your emotions.*

Walking up the path, I feel an overwhelming urge to grab his hand. So much for self-control. I have been fighting the shift in my feelings for him a while now. I can keep fighting them, because the other option isn't even something I want to consider.

"Do I get a hint about what this surprise is?" Alex's voice sends shivers down my spine, it's so sexy.

"You will see shortly." Grinning up at him, I try to ignore the way my heart speeds up. I've been in denial for too long, and apparently my body is refusing to let me hide any more.

Clearing my throat as we arrive at the pen housing Alex's colt and Hoover, I point. "You remember Ryan's colt, Hoover.

The bay horse next to him is yours. I told you I would find the perfect horse, and I was in here playing with them when he caught my eye. I've been spending some time with him to ensure he's the right one, and he is."

Alex watches the colt for a few minutes without saying anything. A lump forms in my throat, I had expected excitement, not silence.

I didn't sleep at all last night. Tossing and turning as I thought about the past ten months getting to know Alex, especially over these last several weeks. Not seeing him yesterday made me realize how accustomed I am to being with him.

"He's perfect." Alex links his fingers with mine, the smile he has just for me pushes away my doubt. "Tell me about him."

My eyes are still locked on our joined hands, my brain reading too much into the gesture, so it takes me a moment to respond. I have to talk myself off the "falling for my fuck buddy" ledge before I can speak.

When I feel like my emotions are under control, I look up at Alex, praying he can't read what's going on in my head.

"Well, he's sweet and gentle. He's easy going just like you, and I've done some work with the colts, he is smart and has been very eager to learn. He's one year old, which means we can do some basic groundwork, which I've started." He smiles as I talk, taking pleasure in my excitement. Horses are my passion. Ever since I was a little girl, helping Papa around the ranch, I knew I wanted to work with horses.

"Good thing I have the best trainer, I have no doubt he will be perfect for me."

Alex drops my hand and climbs the fence, walking over to meet his horse. Flexing my hand, I climb the fence after him. "I never thought this would happen. I go from hardly riding to having my own horse. You're corrupting me."

Grinning, I follow closely behind him, watching as he

cautiously reaches out the rub his colt's neck. "What are you going to name him?"

Alex steps in closer, looking at him carefully. I should be watching the horse, but my eyes are locked on Alex's face and the way his eyes shine. "Leo."

Leo leans into him, enjoying the scratches. "That's perfect." Moving in close to stand next to him, I scratch Leo behind the ears. "Oh, I have something for you. Another present, I guess."

Running over to the gate, I unhook the halter and lead rope I bought for him. It is burgundy red and looks stunning on Leo. Handing it to Alex, the look on his face would make it seem like I gave him something more than a halter.

"Wow. Thank you." He looks amazed when Leo lets him put the halter on and starts following him as he walks. "I feel so spoiled."

"Don't worry about it. You help us a ton around here, this is the least we can do." Alex looks down at me, his hazel eyes warm. Before I can stop myself, I grab his neck and pull him in for a kiss.

This kiss is different than our usual kisses, it's slow and sensuous without the expected end result of sex. Moaning as his tongue brushes against mine, I wind my arms behind his neck enjoying the slow, exploratory pace.

Warmth spreads through my body, I don't think I will ever get tired of the way he kisses me. I feel sexy, and desired, and like I'm the only person he sees in the world. This kiss isn't one meant to lead anywhere, but it's the kind of kiss that makes you fall in love. Something I realize I've been doing since before we came to this agreement. I'm so screwed.

Alex's arms wrap around me, holding me close. It's one of those hugs that puts you back together if you're falling apart, all it does to me is remind me that I've allowed myself to fall for someone who doesn't want me that way. Right now he's putting me back together, but it won't be long until he's tearing me apart.

Reluctantly I pull away, both of us breathing heavily. He looks at me questioningly and I know he can read the confusion on my face, so I gesture to Leo. "Let's take him to the barn. Actually, I will grab Hoover and we will take them both. I don't want Hoover to get upset and they've become buddies."

The walk back to the barn is uncomfortably quiet. In the short time I've known Alex, I've never felt uncomfortable around him. My brain works double time trying to figure out how to fix this. Usually being around Alex calms the whirlwind that is my train of thought, right now he's having the opposite effect. I know it has everything to do with the realization I've come to, and the fact it means I need to make a decision about how far I'm going to allow this to go.

We lead the horses into the barn, putting them in stalls for the night.

As we pass an empty stall, I shove Alex inside, grinding my body into him, fisting my hands in his hair and kissing him roughly. He moans into me, deepening the kiss as his tongue strokes mine. The awkwardness melts away as we fall into our routine struggle to master each other. Pulling back, I grasp his erection through his jeans, and smirk at the desire in his eyes. This is what we need, to reset our relationship to what works.

I can handle this.

Alex looks around before we frantically strip down, he lifts me and presses me against the wall. Wrapping my legs around him, we move together harmoniously. Using his shoulders as leverage, I lift myself up and drop down, his cock slamming into me just right.

My back bangs into the wall of the stall, marking my skin with the force of our passion. His hands squeeze my hips, leaving indents as he murmurs to me.

I have no idea what he's saying, but the husky tone of his voice tells me he's close. Reaching between us, I rub my clit until my muscles start contracting. Clenching around him, I cry out as we find our release at the same time. Fast, hard, and head spinning.

"Wow." Resting my forehead against his, I feel relieved that the awkwardness has passed. Kissing him lightly, I drop my legs as he lowers me to the ground. Leaning against the wall, I watch him cover up his magnificent body.

He sees me staring, smirking as I turn quickly to do up my bra.

"Why don't you come have supper with Emma and me tonight? She invited me over, she thinks we need a weekly dinner since we're not living together anymore." His offer surprises me and I need to compose myself before turning. "Emma had mentioned you're heading over there for girls night, you might as well eat real food before the junk you two love to fill up on."

"That sounds nice." Stepping out of the stall, I smile. "And probably a good idea. The last time I woke up feeling sick from the crash of the sugar high I was on."

The scent of whatever Emma is cooking slams into me, my stomach gurgling in appreciation. Alex wasn't in his room, so I assumed he came over here earlier to work with Emma. Despite setting up an office at the house, more often than not he comes to sit in his spot next to her on the couch.

Following my nose to the kitchen, I'm shocked when I see Alex in the kitchen, cooking, and Emma seated at the breakfast bar, glass of wine in hand.

"You have him trained well." Winking at Emma, I gratefully accept the glass of wine Alex hands me.

Sitting in the stool next to Emma, I turn to my best friend. "Sorry I've been such a shitty friend."

"What the hell are you talking about? I see you every day." She elbows me in the side, her expression scolding.

"We haven't had girl's night in over a month. Besides, with breakfast, everyone is there, and we can't talk about them." Alex turns, arching his brow at us. "Ugh, why can everyone do that except me?" Scowling as they laugh at me, I try to arch my brow only causing them to laugh even harder as my face contorts in every way except the way I want it to.

He turns back to the stove, shutting off the burner. "I made chili, I hope that's okay."

"What would you do if we said no?" I can't resist teasing him and I notice Emma watching us. I've already decided to tell her what's going on after Alex leaves. I need my best friend, and she knows him better than anyone.

Alex laughs without responding to my question, handing Emma and I bowls.

We serve ourselves and sit at the small kitchen table. Tasting my first bite, I ignore the pain as I burn my tongue, the burst of flavors overwhelming it.

"This is so good!" Emma voices her approval before digging in vigorously.

Blowing gently on my spoonful, I see Alex watching me, his expression heated. Glancing at Emma, I see she is focused on her food, so I lick my lower lip and watch him as I wrap my lips around the spoon. He swallows, watching my mouth.

The sound of the front door shutting distracts him as we watch the entrance to the kitchen, waiting to see who it is.

"Do you have room for one more? I finished earlier than I expected." Dane steps into the kitchen, sniffing appreciatively.

Grabbing a bowl, he helps himself and sits next to Emma. The love in their eyes as Dane leans over to kiss her is the stuff of movies.

The reflection of the four of us in the window catches my eye. We look like two couples enjoying dinner. Dropping my eyes, I focus on my chili rather than the feeling of disappointment that the picture in the window isn't my reality.

Dinner passes quickly with easy chatter. I avoid looking in the window again, focusing on enjoying my friend's company. The guys excuse themselves, heading to Linger for guys night. Emma and I shoving them out the door, insisting we would do the dishes.

Back in the kitchen, Emma fills the sink with water.

"I'm so glad we've finally made time to do this. Dane is forcing me to take a few days off since I jumped from one book straight into another."

"You should have time off. Play with Arwen, or read a book."

She hands me a plate, and as I dry it I can't hold in my thoughts any longer.

"Em . . . I need to tell you something."

Emma hangs up the dishcloth, before sitting on the counter facing me. "This sounds serious."

"It's just, I don't want you to freak out or get mad." Smiling guiltily, I blurt it out. "Alex and I have been having sex for over a month now."

Her jaw drops in disbelief, before excitement fills her eyes. "You're serious? That's so great! Why didn't you tell us you're a couple?"

"Well, you see, we're not. We're just sleeping together. It's just lately, I dunno, I've been feeling more. It's kind of snuck up on me over the past few days and I couldn't keep this from you anymore. I'm curious . . . I know you said Alex doesn't have serious relationships, nothing that actually has the chance of lasting. Do you think that could change?" Staring at my hands, I can feel the smile beaming towards me. "You're going to break your face with that grin."

"I knew it! I so called that something was going on." Emma hops down from the counter to stand in front of me, forcing me to look at her. "I think he will change. You're a one of a kind person, Lia, and if I believe anyone can break through to him, it's you. Just be patient. He's weird about relationships, but after my parents passed away he's gotten even more rigid about his boundaries. Sometimes it's easy to forget everything he has gone through, he doesn't trust easily and I think that's a big hindrance for him."

"I know. He hasn't really told me anything about his past. We've been hanging out more, and we have fun. I was a fool to think I could leave feelings out of this."

She looks at me, not letting my eyes drop. "You're in love with him."

Unable to deny it, I nod, mortified when tears start to fill my eyes. "I think a part of me fell for him the first time I saw him. Angry and ready to defend your honor." Closing my eyes, I whisper, "He's going to break my heart when he finds out."

"You never know. All you need is a little hope. I've been watching how Alex looks at you, I don't think he's as immune to deeper feelings that you think he is. He might just need time to sort it out. If you can give him that, then just keep showing him how easy it is with you."

She hops off the counter and wraps her arms around me.

"Just hold on to hope." I murmur. "I can try to do that."

# CHAPTER NINE

*Lia*

A soft knock on the door to my clinic draws my attention from the article I'm reading. I try to stay on top of new therapy techniques, going to seminars at least twice a year and reading all of the latest research.

A petite woman stands in the doorway, her dark eyes nervous as she watches me stand from my desk. Her dark hair is tied back in a ponytail, her face is clear of makeup, and as I examine her, I can see a haunted look in her eyes. My heart breaks that someone so young looks so broken.

"Hello, I'm Lia Hyatt. I'm sorry, in the shock of Georgiana's request, I forgot to get your name." Reaching my hand out there is a pause before she cautiously slides her hand into mine. Her handshake is firm, despite her nervousness.

"Nella Anderson. Thank you for letting me come." She steps into the room, standing awkwardly as I shut the door. "I don't know if Ms. Waters told you, but I've never been around horses before."

Gesturing to one of the armchairs in the room, I sit across from her and fold my legs underneath my butt. "That's okay. This afternoon I have two new horses coming. I thought you could help me with them from start to finish. This morning, we'll tour the facility and we can get you acquainted with being around horses. First, if you don't mind, I'd like to learn just a little about you, and I need you to sign a waiver."

"Okay." She nods, before eyeing me cautiously. "What do you want to know?"

I smile reassuringly. It's obvious she's worried that I'm going to ask why Ms. Waters sent her to me, but her journey is her own and I refuse to pry. "What are you studying?"

"I just finished my second year. I'm working towards my Bachelor of Science. My major is Biology, and my minor is Psychology." She mimics my pose on the chair as she relaxes slightly.

"Wow, those two don't normally go together." She grins, causing me to smile in response.

"Biology is because I love it. Psychology because the way the human mind works fascinates me." She shrugs, playing with the frayed ends of her jeans. "I don't have a plan for when I'm done. I haven't found anything that calls to me yet."

"You have time. Sometimes you need to try a few things before you figure out what you want." Standing from the chair, I grab her file off my desk and hand it to her. "Let's get the boring paperwork out of the way, and then I will show you around."

Nella fills in the information form. Emergency contacts, allergies, contact info, before signing the release. She looks up at me. "There is nothing here about cost."

"I'm not charging you, or the school. The way I look at it,

you will be helping me immensely with the horses and we can see where it goes."

She tucks the pen in the file, handing it to me.

"Your contacts, no family?" I ask after a quick perusal, careful to keep my tone neutral.

She shakes her head. "No, they're far away. I put my roommate and my best friend. They are close and more reliable."

I toss her file back on my desk, smiling encouragingly. "Are you ready for the grand tour?"

She eagerly pushes off the chair, making me grin.

I lead her out through the barn, introducing her to the horses. Her eyes widen when we get to the pool. "Holy shit."

We walk through the pool area back into the barn and head into the small arena.

"I do a bunch of different treatments. Primarily chiropractic and massage. However, some of the horse's blocks are more mental. They've had a traumatic experience, so I do investigative work to find their triggers and try to work them through it." We walk outside so I can introduce her to the rest of the horses in the paddocks.

Leading her to where Ollie is grazing, I open the gate and wait as she walks past me, her face a combination of excitement and nervousness. "This is my horse, Ollie. I think we will start each day with horsemanship and riding lessons. In order for you to feel comfortable around the treatment horses, you will need to have an understanding of horse behavior."

We spend the rest of the morning going over basic awareness when interacting with horses. Body language, setting boundaries, how to approach a horse properly, and by the time we stop for lunch, I'm thoroughly impressed at how quickly Nella is picking up on everything.

Walking back into my clinic, I can't hold back the smile when I see Alex sitting in my office chair.

"Nella, this is Alex. Alex, Nella." I leave the room to grab the food I packed for us from the fridge in my living quarters. Nella is curled back up on the arm chair as I hand her the salad I made. "Nella is a natural with the horses."

She flushes at the compliment, looking pleased with herself. As she should.

Popping the lid on my container, I smile warmly at the girl sitting opposite me before taking a bite of the chicken Caesar salad. She ducks her head, smiling shyly as she eats.

"I wasn't expecting to see you this afternoon." Setting my container down, I glance over at Alex.

He grins, making my heart stutter. Now that I've admitted my feelings, my body has gone into overdrive whenever he's around. I already reacted strongly to him, but adding emotion to it has been overwhelming.

"I forgot that you had company today." His meaning implied, I can't help the disappointment at the fact he was here for a booty call and not just to see me. "Since you're busy, maybe we could go for dinner tonight."

"Like, out? Or at the house?" Frowning, I scold myself for being hopeful. Despite what Emma said, hope leads to disappointment.

"Out." He stands from the chair, walks around the desk and sits on the arm of the chair I'm in, looking down at me.

"Okay. I should be done here around four, and I will need time to get ready." He leans down and presses his lips against mine in a soft kiss. When he pulls away, I know the surprise on his face is reflected on my own.

"See you at six then." He says goodbye to Nella, and is out the door leaving a chaos of emotions in his wake.

Shaking it off, I take Nella's empty container and clean up. Our client is expected at one, so I go over the new client paperwork with Nella, aware of her curious eyes on me.

"That's complicated." I supply, my eyes on the closed door of my office.

She nods, her eyes flashing with awareness. I'm pretty sure she sees right through me, but she doesn't comment.

Alex helps me out of my coat, his fingertips brushing down my bare arms as he removes it leaving a trail of goosebumps. Draping it over my chair, he waits until I'm seated before sitting across from me. I've been a nervous wreck from the moment I stepped out the door and got into his truck.

The drive here was filled with our normal conversation, and I'm proud of myself for not letting my nerves show.

This is a date, our first. We may not have put the words to it, but the restaurant Alex chose is romantic. The low lighting, earthy tones, and soft jazzy music complete the atmosphere. Looking around, it's all couples seated around us.

I feel the hope I've been trying to control flare again. Damn Emma for telling me what I want isn't impossible.

"You look beautiful." Alex reaches across the table, stroking his fingertips over the top of my hand.

"What are we doing Alex?" The question is out before I can stop it, his fingers freezing on the top of my hand. Understanding his motives is the only way I can shield myself. I'm already going to shatter if things go south, and this just complicates things. My feelings are outside my control at this point, but Alex is the one holding our agreement together, and now he's blurring the already faded lines.

"What do you mean?" He pulls his hand back, picking up the menu. I can see him shut down before me, but I press on.

"This is a date." Leaning back, I watch him as the server fills our water glasses and take our drink order. When the man leaves, I lean forward again, folding my hands in my lap. "I'm not saying I mind, I'm just curious if you're attempting to change the parameters of our relationship."

He looks at me over the menu, heat flaring in his eyes at my bluntness.

"One of the things I like about you Lia, is that you don't let me get away with shit, however this is nothing more than me wanting to spend time with you. Nothing is changing, but I wanted a chance to be with my friend while treating her as my lover." He turns back to his menu, unaware of the disappointment surging through me.

My mind rebels against his words, but I bite my tongue. He can deny it all he wants, but this is a fucking date. His words are basically the definition of what a date means.

Maybe it's time to show him that what we have is a relationship, there is no point in denying it any longer. The only difference between our relationship and the other couples here, is that our family and friends don't know. Well, in theory.

Man, he would be pissed if he knew Emma and Ryan know what's going on. I should tell him at some point, but for right now I'm going to enjoy our first real date.

"How did it go with Nella today?" Alex picks up his wine, studying me as he takes a sip.

It's obvious he is watching my reaction over our exchange. He relaxes as I start to tell him about my day, obviously I'm getting better at masking my feelings. I've never been one to shy away from telling people exactly how I feel, but I need to show Alex how I feel and that it can work rather than tell him.

"I really like her. If the rest of the summer continues to go well, I am thinking about offering her a job. She doesn't know what she wants for a career, but if this is something she enjoys and she doesn't mind living out here, then it's something I would consider."

Our server comes back to take our orders, disappearing as quickly as he did the first time. I like that they don't hover and try to make small talk.

"I didn't realize you wanted help." Alex leans forward, his eyes intent on mine.

"I've thought about it, but the person would have to be just the right fit. It would be nice to have someone trained on what to do, especially since I'm out of town a lot for horse shows." I absently play with the stem of my wine glass, watching the way Alex's eyes follow the movement of my fingers. "Speaking of horse shows, my first one is next weekend. Jesse is coming to stay at the house to look after everything. Between us, I think he's looking forward to a break from Ashton. Anyways, everyone is coming to cheer me on for the weekend if you want to join us. It's only an hour away, but we like to camp out and visit."

"Yeah, I will come. It'll be fun watching you compete."

I smile at him, his returning grin turning my insides to mush. Thankfully, the server comes back with our dinner, so I'm able to break eye contact before I give myself away.

Digging into my Creole Chicken, I take a moment to gather my thoughts. Sometimes the way my brain works gives me whiplash. One moment I'm in denial, the next I've accepted I've fallen for this man. This is how it always goes for me. It takes me time to sort through the chaos in my head, but once I've muddled my way through I don't bother living in the state of denial.

I watch him eat, enjoying being out with him and not needing to pretend nothing is going on. He smiles at me, his eyes heating. As he leans forward to say something, his phone dings with a text. A glance down, and the smile is gone, replaced with a frown.

"What's wrong?" Alex rarely frowns. He's the guy who

walks around with a smile on his face. Incredible considering what he's gone through.

"My mother texted me again. She insists that she's sober and wants to see me." He runs his fingers through his hair as he shuts his phone off without responding. "The woman spent the better part of two years drunk and high. Taking out her frustrations on me, and she wonders why the hell I don't fucking want to see her. Give me a freakin' break."

His chest heaves as he vents his frustration. It's obvious he feels guilty for not giving her the chance, but who could blame him.

"Alex." His eyes fly to mine as he realizes what he just unleashed. I hold his gaze, thinking through my next words carefully. "A parent is more than the person who gave birth to you. A parent is the person who keeps you safe, who you know you can count on. She may be your mother, but you don't owe her anything. Your parents were Emma's. They may have come into your life when you were twelve, but they stepped up in a way your parents failed. So if you don't want to talk to her, if you don't want her in your life, no one can fault you that."

He doesn't say anything, but we are locked in each other's eyes until the server comes back to pick up our now empty plates.

"Are you interested in seeing our dessert menu?"

Alex answers before I can, his eyes still locked on mine with heated intensity. "Just the check please. We will be having dessert at home."

The poor man coughs, his fair skin flushing at Alex's meaning before he turns away. To his credit, he's back with the bill in less than a minute. Within five minutes, we're in the car and on our way home.

The drive home is quiet, both of us eager to be in each

other's arms. I've been wet ever since he told the waiter we were having dessert at home.

Shifting in the seat, I glare at Alex's knowing smirk. "This is your fault."

Licking my lips, I reach my hand over and slide my hand over Alex's thigh, before cupping his erection in my hand. He swallows as I undo his button and slide my hand inside his jeans and boxer briefs.

Wrapping my fingers around his cock, I stroke him, enjoying the soft skin beneath my fingers. His smirk is gone as he speeds up, his hands clenched around the steering wheel as I work my hand from base to tip.

With a growl, he pulls my hand away before turning into our driveway. Throwing the car in park, he doesn't bother doing up his pants before he's out of the car. He shuts my door behind me, picks me up and stalks into the house.

Peering over my shoulder, I grin when I see Emma sitting on her porch watching us. I love that I've made him forget to be cautious, that he loses himself so entirely in me that he forgets we're not alone.

Pressing my lips to his neck, I breathe him in.

Maybe it's not hopeless.

# CHAPTER TEN

*Alex*

My eyes burst open, my skin coated in a light sheen of sweat from the dream I was having. Lia moans softly, curling into me as she sleeps.

Watching her sleep, her face soft and slightly flushed, calms the thundering race of my heart. I wrap my arms around her and hold her close, letting her presence pull me away from the nightmare. It's been a long time since I've been plagued by the dreams, but Mom has texted me three more times since the night I had dinner with Lia.

I haven't responded, Lia's words reminding me that I have no reason to feel guilty, but she's decided to persist, which is unusual.

Freezing when my door bursts open, Emma comes bounding into my room looking far too energized for the early hour. She doesn't even falter at seeing Lia in my arms as she sits on the edge of my bed.

"Shit. I can explain." I shift Lia away from me, feeling the loss of her heat as she rolls away from us, curling onto her side with a soft murmur. I doubt Emma will care that I'm sleeping with Lia, she will care more that I've been hiding it from her. Emma looks at me with humor in her eyes. "You don't seem to be that surprised."

"I saw you the other night, carrying her from your car like a caveman. Anyways, look what I found in the attic." She hands me a photo I hadn't seen in her hand.

Scanning it, I do a double take when I see her father and my mother with a group of people I don't recognize. My mom looks young and vibrant. Happy. I try to recall a time when she looked like that, but there was always an overtone of sadness to her that is absent in the photo.

"On the back it gives the date. Apparently they hung out with the same group of friends in college. This photo was taken a couple of months before my dad met my mom." She takes the photo back, looking down on it. "I wonder why he never said anything when we moved in next door."

"Who knows? Maybe because my father made it apparent he wanted nothing to do with your parents. My mom blamed them for his leaving, you know that."

"Oh yeah, I forgot about that." Looking at the picture, her brows crease. "She looks so different than I remember her."

We sit silently, looking at the picture. I don't think I ever saw my mother as happy as she is in the photo. Even looking back to when things were okay with my parents.

Emma stands from my bed, glancing over at Lia with a smug look on her face. "Well, I will let you get back to your morning. We're heading for the show at three. Ryan is going to join us tomorrow so the four of us will drive together."

She prances out of the room, shutting the door quietly behind her. Groaning, I run a hand over my face. Looking over at Lia, I ignore the way my body reacts to her. It's no longer just physical, I enjoy every moment we spend together. This thing has become very real, and I don't know how to deal.

Lia yawns, her brown eyes blinking up at me sleepily. "Good morning."

Her smile is soft, unguarded, and the look in her eyes hits me in the gut. Shit. I've noticed her fighting me less and less for control, but right now, as she wakes up, I see what she's been hiding from me.

This is no longer casual for her either. My throat closes up as I fight for air, that realization rendering me speechless.

She sits up, the sheets tucked under her arms, her mask falling into place as she waits for me to say something. Her gaze hasn't left mine.

Wrapping my hand around the back of her neck, I pull her down and kiss her softly. Part of me wants her to leave so I can process how to deal with what's going on, the other part doesn't want her to go, because while she's here the panic I feel waiting in the background will stay away.

"Do you think we can skip breakfast? I have plans for you this morning." Trailing a finger down her arm, I smirk.

"As much as I would love to spend all morning in bed with you, I need to finish getting ready for the show." She pulls away, but runs her fingers through my hair and kisses me before crawling out of bed.

I sit against the headboard as I watch her dress, shooting me a smile as she opens the door and runs across the hall.

Before the panic can flood my system, a sharp knock sounds on my door before it swings in revealing Ryan. He looks behind him, listening for a moment, before returning his gaze to mine. Leaning against the doorframe, he crosses his arms.

"I like you, so you need to think long and hard this

weekend about what it is you want from my baby sister. If this is only a fling, then end it now before you break her heart." He pushes off the frame, with one last withering look taps the top of the doorway and is down the hall before I can form a coherent thought.

By the time we all load into Emma's truck, I'm exhausted. I know I need to think shit through, but I'm not ready to process that the agreement I have with Lia needs to come to an end. So, instead of dealing with the issue like an adult, I worked out for an hour with music blasting in my ears, I packed for the week-end, rode Chandler, and finally signed off on the website that has been a thorn in my side for close to two months.

"So how do these shows work?" Leaning back in the truck, I settle in for a long drive. An hour is nothing, but whenever I look at Lia all I can see is the love that was shining from her eyes this morning. It makes my heart stop, before taking off at a thundering pace in my chest.

"This afternoon the arena will be open to practicing. Any rider that wants can go inside to work their horses. Out of courtesy, we practice the same thing and then switch it up. There are also paid warmups. I have one this evening and one tomorrow before the classes start." Lia angles herself on the bench seat, tucking a leg underneath her. "There are different classes depending on the level of the rider. I have two classes I'm riding in. The Open class tomorrow, and the Freestyle class on Sunday."

"It's a pretty casual atmosphere. We'll be in the warm-up area cheering Lia on." Dane turns in his seat. "The base score, with no mistakes but also nothing outstanding, is seventy per judge. There are three judges and their scores are combined for the final score. You can gain or lose points depending on how you ride."

It sounds easy enough to follow. I've been watching Lia practice this week, learning what the judges look for as Ryan shouted corrections to her. It's going to be tough watching Ollie's movements and not focusing on the intent look on Lia's face, there is something intensely attractive when she is focused on the pattern and the movement of her body.

Dane turns back to face the windshield, striking up a conversation with Emma. Looking to my left, I catch Lia watching me with a thoughtful look on her face. I've caught that look on her face several times throughout the day, whenever we've crossed paths. It makes me wonder if my feelings are as transparent to her as hers are to me.

She hasn't confronted me about my moment of panic, or the obvious fear that's been bubbling under the surface since this morning, which makes me even more nervous because Lia doesn't shy away from confrontation.

The rest of the drive passes quickly, and soon we've parked the trailer and settled Ollie into his stall. The commotion around us is fascinating. Several people call out to Lia, greeting her. This is a part of her life I've never experienced. Last summer, I never went to any of her shows, too distracted by everything going on with Emma.

Leaning against Ollie's stall, I watch Lia set up a temporary tack room. Emma and Dane went to town to pick up some last minute supplies, leaving us alone. I still haven't thought through what I'm going to do. I want Lia to enjoy her weekend and, if I'm being honest, I don't want this to end quite yet, but seeing the affection in her eyes this morning, the unguarded look that told me she's falling for me, brought reality crashing down. No matter what happens now, when this ends, it's going to hurt her.

Lia steps out of the stall she's using as a tack room, shutting it and dropping a curtain I didn't notice her hang across the front. It boasts the name of her practice, alongside her contact info.

As she turns to look at me, she's suddenly lifted in the air, being hugged from behind.

"I knew it felt hotter in here," a voice rumbles out from the face buried in her hair and I'm frozen with the rage that surges through me.

The dude sets her back on the ground, spinning her around. His cowboy hat shields his face from me as he looks down on her. I want to fucking rip his hands away from her body, drag her to the horse trailer and bury myself deep inside of her until she forgets everyone's name but mine.

She giggles at something cowboy has said, my hands fisting at the sound. That's my fucking giggle. Stalking to stand next to her, cowboy finally looks up at me.

Of course, he looks like fucking Scott Eastwood. Emma made me watch that damn rodeo movie several times swooning over him, and here is his doppelganger with one hand still resting on Lia's hip.

Lia glances up at me, her face flushed. "Dominic, this is Alex. Alex, Dominic."

Cowboy holds his hand out to me, shaking firmly before dropping it.

"I gotta go, gorgeous, but I will see you in the arena." He bends to drop a kiss on her cheek, before turning on the heel of his boot and heading out of the barn.

Before my head has time to catch up with my body, I've grabbed Lia's hand and I'm dragging her to the trailer.

Opening the door to the living quarters, I lift her inside before shutting and locking the door behind me.

Threading my fingers through her hair, I tilt her head back and kiss her. Every ounce of my rage and jealousy is thrown into the kiss. It's hard, and punishing, but she opens up to me giving back just as good as she gets.

Until Lia, a kiss was always just a kiss, but with her it's every unspoken word that hangs between us. I can feel her love pouring into me, while my response is pure, primal possessiveness.

Dropping my hands to her waist, I hold on tight trying to imprint myself into her as we let our bodies speak the words we both refuse to say.

Pulling away, I strip her shirt off, her bra joining it on the floor, before I pull off her boots and remove her jeans. She leans against the table, watching as I remove my own clothes.

We haven't spoken one word, I can't right now, because I know I will say something I can't take back.

Turning her, I plant her hands on the table angling her body so her breasts are pressed down on the surface. She presses back into me, moaning as I drive into her. She's fucking soaked, her pussy clenching around my cock as I move in and out of her in fast, hard motions.

It's rough, urgent, and primal. Every ounce of my energy is going into making her forget that asshole who made her giggle and flush. Next time she sees him, I don't want her to remember his name, I want her to remember how I feel inside of her.

Stilling inside her as she clenches my cock, the force of her orgasm making her legs shake, I follow close behind, spilling into her as I come harder than I think I've ever come before.

Pulling out, I cross the short distance to the bathroom and wet a cloth. Lia is still bent over the table, so I gently clean her up before tending to myself. I quickly use the facilities, giving myself a moment to come down from the high, and when I come out Lia is fully dressed with her boots back in place.

She presses into me, lifting onto her toes and kissing me with a softness that contradicts the rough way I just took her.

We still haven't said a word, and before I can she is slipping out the door, closing it with a quiet click.

I dress, my mind going haywire. I have never been jealous like that, ever. Even when I kissed her in front of Graham, it wasn't out of jealousy, although the need that night had been just as primal as just now.

I'm addicted to Lia's body, but not just that, I'm also addicted to her smile and her passion for her job. I'm addicted to making her giggle, and talking with her about everything. The fear I've been suppressing all day rises, but I tamp it down again.

I know I need to end this before any more emotions get involved, but not until after the weekend is done. Things have gotten too real for me.

My stomach turns over just at the thought of ending this. Obviously there are men out there who would jump on the chance for something more, and the idea of witnessing it makes me ill.

Stepping out of the trailer, Emma is sitting in a lawn chair watching me descend the steps with a knowing smirk.

Before she can say anything, I inquire, "Where'd Lia and Dane go?"

"They're getting Ollie ready. The arena opens in five minutes for the open practice. I was waiting for you, we will meet them there." She stands from her chair, and I know she is going to say something.

"Don't." Cutting her off before she has the chance, I raise my hand in front of me.

"I'm just going to say one thing."

*I should have known.*

"I know that look in your eyes. It's the one you always get before you drop whatever woman you have in your life. Think carefully through that decision before you screw up something that has been making you happier than I've ever known you." She doesn't wait for me to respond, turning and walking toward the entrance of the huge building behind us.

I follow silently, stewing over the information overload from today. I must've been blind not to notice any of it sooner, but right now I feel like I'm drowning in the torrent of my thoughts.

We find Dane in the mass of people and horses. There is a small warm up area where riders wait for someone to clear out of the competition arena where they are practicing. Lia is already inside, loping circles.

I can't believe the number of people they allow in there, and I'm even more impressed by the fact no one crashes. My jaw snaps shut when I see Dominic ride up alongside Lia, saying something to her that makes her laugh.

Emma chuckles softly beside me. Instead of responding, I elbow her in the side, not taking my eyes off Lia.

Dane growls when Dominic leans over to tuck a strand of hair behind Lia's ear. "If he's in there to pick up women, he should have gone to a fucking bar."

Emma laughs, but I'm happy someone is on my side.

"He's sexy, and they have a lot in common. I can't say I'm surprised that he's taken an interest." She looks up at me, a challenge clear in her eyes. She doesn't need to say the words. If I don't want anything serious with Lia, I should step down so someone else can have a shot.

"Not Cowboy Casanova over there. He just wants someone to fuck once in a while before moving on. Lia needs someone who can be serious about her, she deserves that after the shit she's dealt with. Lia is the type of woman you fall in love and settle down with, nothing less is worth her time."

My stomach turns over at Dane's words. Emma wraps her fingers around mine, squeezing. I know what she wants from me, what she believes I'm capable of giving, but I don't think I can do it.

# CHAPTER ELEVEN

**Lia**

*He knows.*

It's barely the ass-crack of dawn and I'm awake. Alex has been acting strangely since yesterday morning, a little distant, and definitely more guarded. And it's because he knows I'm in love with him.

He didn't drop his guard until Dominic was flirting with me, and his response was one of instinct rather than thought. It was like his mind shut down and his body took over.

As soon as he pulled me inside the trailer, I also realized what he hasn't yet. He loves me too. I just wish his head would catch up to his heart and his body.

Sighing, I roll out of bed and dress. Brushing my teeth, I scowl when I see the bags under my eyes. Emma and Dane took the big bed, Alex is on the couch, so I ended up on the tiny bed the table folds down into. It wasn't the most comfortable night's sleep I've ever had. All I wanted was to crawl into bed with Alex, having him so close was torture.

Everyone is still sleeping, so I grab a protein bar and slip out of the trailer. I need to get to the warm-up ring anyways. My paid warm-up is in forty-five minutes and I don't want to spend fifteen of that moving Ollie through his stretches.

It doesn't take me long to groom and tack Ollie, but Ryan is waiting for me in the pen when I lead him in there. Stepping into his arms, I hug him tightly. "When are Mom and Dad coming?"

"They will be here for your first class."

I'm so grateful to have such a supportive family, especially after hearing some of the shit Alex had to go through. It makes me appreciate them so much more. Not that I didn't already, Dom is here every show without anyone to cheer him on or keep him company, and he does it with a smile on his face.

Ryan sits in one of the seats alongside the fence as I swing myself into the saddle. I love having the first paid warm-up, no one else is in here. It's quiet and it gives me time to push every thought from my head aside from Ollie and the show. Something I definitely need today.

My thoughts swirl around Alex and everything that has happened between us over the past couple of months. I know what I want, but I don't think continuing as we are will help him realize he wants the same things. He's conditioned himself to avoid commitment, and if I try to push him into something it will just drive him away.

"Lia, you need to focus. Get your mind on your horse. Use your seat and be the competitor I know you can be." Ryan's voice is harsh, drawing me from my thoughts.

He's right, I need to get into the mindset and I can figure out everything after.

Stopping Ollie, I hold my hand up as Ryan starts to speak. "Let me find my center."

Closing my eyes, I breathe deeply until everything falls away. Focusing on the rhythmic feel of Ollie breathing under me, the way he shifts his weight, I sink into my seat and think about the pattern. I think about the way the slightest touch from my legs tells Ollie exactly what I need from him.

By the time I open my eyes, the noise from everything else is gone. I can feel my forehead crease with determination, and even when I notice that Emma, Dane, and Alex have joined Ryan, I don't lose my focus.

"Paid warm-up, Lia Hyatt riding Smokin' Guns Ammo, owner, Lia Hyatt."

Turning away from my family and friends, I nod at the woman opening the gate for me, loping into the center of the arena.

We move through the pattern flawlessly, and by the time I've exited the arena, a crowd has formed, including Dominic. He waits for me outside the gate, and I grin when I catch Alex watching out of the corner of my eye. I've known Dominic for years. He's a few years older than me, and a hopeless flirt, but I also know he has mad respect for me and his flirting is harmless.

"Gorgeous, as usual." He stands by Ollie's head as I dismount, moving in next to me once my feet are on the ground. "That guy over there, he's your boyfriend, yeah?"

Laughing, I shake my head. "He's . . . complicated."

I glance over at Alex, he's still watching.

"He wants to hurt me." Dominic leans down to whisper in my ear. "I kind of like torturing him. If he has you, it shouldn't be complicated. Even I know you're not the kind of girl a guy lets go, why do you think I haven't snapped you up for myself."

He pulls back with a naughty smirk on his face, and I burst

out laughing. I can see my brothers are now watching us too. They know Dominic's reputation, and I'm sure he has all three of them glowering at him.

Lifting my hand, I rest it on his shoulder and lift on my toes to kiss him on the cheek. "I've missed you. See you later, I'll be the one kicking your ass."

Grabbing Ollie's reins, I walk over to where my crew is standing. I wasn't wrong, Dane and Ryan are glaring at Dominic, while Alex is watching me with the same heat he had yesterday before he fucked me in the trailer. I have slight bruises on my hips to show for it.

Glancing over at Emma, I see she is just standing there grinning at all the testosterone around her.

Before I meet them, she comes over, her eyes glinting. "You naughty, naughty girl."

"I don't know what you're talking about." Smirking, I deny it.

"Uh huh. Normally, I would tell someone not to play with fire, but in this case I'm on board. Besides, Dominic is me-wow." She fans herself, ignoring the way Dane is now glaring at her. I can tell by the looks on their faces they can hear us, and after a moment I realize she meant for that to happen.

"Did you seriously just say me-wow?" We close the rest of the distance to the fence, getting out of the way of the riders who are warming up.

"Yep." She pops her lips on the "p" with a grin.

Dane pulls her into his arms, leaning down to whisper in her ear. I can tell that whatever he's saying is something I don't want to hear by the smile that crosses Emma's face.

"I'm going to cool Ollie down and get him settled. My class is at ten, so I'm going to make the rounds to a few clients before then." Ryan and Alex follow me out, and I can tell that one of them is going to pounce on the Dominic thing.

"Lia." Big brother for the win.

Rolling my eyes, "yes?"

"You shouldn't encourage Dominic's behavior. He's a nice enough guy, but he lacks respect for women." I could lash out, call him a hypocrite. I also think it's funny that he's reading so much into it, considering he knows about Alex, but who can understand the way his mind is working right now?

Sighing, I turn and start walking backwards. Alex is watching me, and the look on his face makes me pause. Instead of anger, which is there, I can also see that he's hurt. Something I didn't expect. I look at Ryan, but my words are for Alex. "Dom has nothing but respect for me. He knows we're friends and nothing more. I've known the guy for six years and he's never tried anything. Besides, I haven't broken my rule about not dating anyone in the show circuit yet."

Shaking my head, I turn back around and speed up. I need a break from all of this, and I know where I need to go to get it.

I can meet up with my clients later.

The comforting smell of leather greets me as I enter The Tack Shop. It's my favorite store, and when I need to clear my head it's my favorite place to get some much needed retail therapy.

"Lia! It's been too long since you've paid us a visit." Megan leans on the counter, her bright smile a balm to my frayed nerves.

"I know. It's a busy time of year."

"That's what you always say. Can I help you find anything?"

Shaking my head, I make my way to the register. "No, I just needed some retail therapy. I have a couple of hours before my class today and I needed some space to think."

"Gotcha." She picks up her phone, her thumb working a mile a minute as she gives me the room I need to breathe.

Despite what I said about thinking, that's the last thing I want to do. I feel like I've spent a ton of time sorting through my feelings and being stuck in my head, so I distract myself by shopping for a new pair of spurs.

An hour and ten text messages later, I've paid for a new set of spurs, new skid boots, and a headstall for Emma's filly.

"Good luck! Not that you need it, Miss Undefeated for three years running." Megan waves to me as I leave, feeling sufficiently soothed.

The only text I bother responding to is Emma's.

Me: Just needed to get away for some quiet time before I show. See you in ten.

Exactly ten minutes later, I'm hopping out of the truck and racing into the trailer. My class starts soon, and I don't want to miss watching any of the riders.

I change into a gorgeous western style button-down shirt. It's simple, only a little bit of flash, but it's a vibrant purple that will stand out. Grabbing my chaps, I leave the trailer. I don't have to ask; Ryan is there helping me zip them up. We secure my cowboy hat with pins to complete the outfit.

"Ollie is ready to go." He knows me. I usually need to leave the chaos of the show before I ride. It gives me the chance to clear my head, and dealing with the Dom issue earlier just fed that need.

"Thanks."

"He's with Mom and Dad in the warm-up pen."

Dane locks the trailer, and everyone walks with me. No one speaks, they just let me pump myself up. Someone must have told Alex I shut down a little before I show, he's giving me the space I need. Have I mentioned how much I appreciate my family and friends?

When we join Mom and Dad, I give them hugs, and lift myself into the saddle. Several people wave to me as I start warming Ollie up.

They call the first rider, prompting the rider after her to be ready. I watch rider after rider run the pattern, walking Ollie to the gate when it's Dom's turn.

He's an excellent rider, but his coach fell ill and couldn't make it. Not that his coach is that great anyways, I've been trying to convince Dom to find someone new, someone more reliable.

Dane and Ryan don't know much about him, aside from what he puts out there, but I know better. He is alone in this world. No one is here to cheer him on outside the normal show crowd. Somehow, along the way, he discovered me and every show he makes sure to spend some time with me so I feel I need to support him however I can.

I call out some encouragement, my voice carrying through the arena. He finishes his pattern with a final score of 213.

I trot Ollie over to wait inside the gate, out of the way of the rider after him, and lift my hand in a high-five.

"Nicely done, Dom."

He smiles, removing his hat and wiping his arm over his forehead. "I wouldn't have done that well if you hadn't been hollering at me. Thanks."

"I'm always in your corner, even if I am going to kick your ass." Dropping Ollie's reins, I stretch in the saddle. They've prompted me that I'm up after they run the tractor over the sand, the harrows it pulls will smooth out the tracks leaving a fresh slate.

"I don't doubt that's true. Good luck. May your tracks be long and true." He winks at me, turning his gelding away.

I position myself in front of the gate, watching the harrows smooth out the tracks from the previous riders. I got the lucky draw, I love going right after the harrows. There is something serene about the smooth ripples in the sand.

Closing my eyes, I find my center, the adrenaline starting to pump through my veins as the tractor leaves and the gates are opened for me.

Cuing Ollie, he takes off, the power of his muscles moving beneath me as we run down the center line. I don't see anything around me, the noise of the crowd sounds more like the rush of running water. The only two beings in the world right now are me and Ollie as I guide him through the pattern.

I love the rush as we fly over the sand, my veins singing with excitement, the pride over every movement executed in perfection lighting me up from the inside out.

As I perform the final maneuver of the pattern, the rest of the world fills back in when I hear the roar of the crowd. Riding over to the judges, I dismount so they can check Ollie over.

They make sure I haven't marked him with my spurs, and ensure the bit in his mouth is the regulation bit. Once they're done, I make my way to the gate and wait for my final score.

"Lia Hyatt on Smokin' Guns Ammo, score two sixteen point five." I wrap my arms around Ollie's neck, not minding the sheen of sweat that covers him. He worked hard today and earned the top score so far.

The roar of the crowd cheering makes me smile. I love how supportive this community of people is. My family and friends swarm me, each one hugging me until I'm wrapped in Alex's arms.

"Wow. That was . . . incredible." He squeezes me tight, pulling back so he can meet my eyes. His shine with excitement from watching me compete and it makes my heart beat a little faster.

"Thank you! I love it. Now, let's go have lunch, I'm starving." Everyone laughs. I stand still so Emma and Ryan can help me out of my chaps and we walk to the barn together, my family leaves to start cooking lunch, but Alex stays behind.

Once Ollie is groomed and settled in for the afternoon, he drops the curtain to my tack room pushing me up against the wall.

"You are so fucking incredible." His voice is low, rumbly. We're very aware of the number of people around us, but it doesn't stop him as he pushes into me and starts kissing me with feverish passion.

He grabs my thighs, lifting me off the ground and wrapping my legs around his lean waist as he devours me. I'm falling apart with every touch, but he puts me back together again. That's what he's done. I hadn't realized how broken I was, my trust in myself ruined because of Graham, but he's stitched me back together so well, you can't even see where the pieces were. I'm whole again, and it's thanks to this beautiful man before me, who was broken just like me.

I hold him tight, giving him everything I have. The difference between us is that he's made me whole again, whereas Alex still holds onto some of the scars from his past. He wears them like an armor he needs to shed, but he's just not ready yet.

My kisses turn desperate, I know he feels the shift, but he doesn't question it. It's too easy for us to ignore what's right there, pretending that nothing has shifted.

I don't know how long we're wrapped up in each other, but

I hear Emma call out for us, so I know it's long enough that lunch is ready.

When Alex lowers me to the ground, he rests his forehead on mine, his eyes searching mine. I can see the flash of pain at what he sees there, but it's gone just as quickly.

He pulls me into his chest, hugging me to him.

We've always had an expiration date, and we both know it's upon us.

# CHAPTER TWELVE

*Alex*

The drive home after the show is quiet. Lia fell asleep within ten minutes of being on the road, her feet resting on my lap. She rode hard, winning both of her classes, so it's not surprising that she's so tired. Not to mention the number of people asking her to help them with their horses. It was staggering. I had no idea she was such an active part of the community, and everyone likes her because she is so kind-hearted and friendly.

I didn't think I would enjoy being a part of this as much as I have, but I like seeing every facet of her life. It's just flowed so easily, I didn't realize how much she has integrated into my everyday life.

Running my hand over her shin, I enjoy the smoothness of her skin against my palm.

Emma turns up the radio a little, her and Dane chatting quietly about the wedding plans they've finally made. Once

Lia suggested the barn for the venue, the rest has fallen into place.

Tuning out their conversation, I watch Lia sleep. She looks so at peace and she's never been so beautiful to me. She deserves so much more than someone like me, Dane hit it on the head yesterday; Lia needs someone who will fall in love with her.

Someone who was taught how to truly love someone, unconditionally.

That little voice that whispers in the back of my brain, the one that tells me I'm making excuses because I'm scared. I'm scared of opening myself up to the possibility of loving someone so much that they can hurt me. Like my dad did, and my mom.

The voice that taunts me for running scared.

Emma parks the truck in front of one of the small paddocks attached to the barn. Lia startles awake when Emma and Dane hop out of the truck, shutting the doors with a loud click.

"Shit. I'm ready to crash." She pulls her feet off my lap, slipping them into flip flops.

Dane already has Ollie unloaded by the time I join them, Lia taking his lead and letting him loose into the pen. She latches his halter on the gate, turning back to face us.

"Leave the trailer. I will clean it tomorrow, right now I just want to eat and go to sleep. Thanks for coming and cheering me on." She hugs Emma and Dane, before walking alongside me to the house.

"Why don't you go take a relaxing shower, get comfy, and I will cook dinner." Shutting the front door behind her, I lean down to brush my lips across hers.

"Sounds perfect." She wraps me in her arms, tucking her face into my chest. I hug her close, a feeling of melancholy filling me when she pulls away too soon, heading up the stairs.

By the time Lia joins me in the kitchen, her wet hair in a knot on the top of her head, I've set the table and dinner is waiting.

She's eyes the plate I've dished out for her hungrily. Her mom must have stopped by before we got home, dropping off a delicious pasta salad. I grilled some chicken and asparagus, seasoned to perfection.

"Oh my God. This looks amazing." She sits down, cutting into her chicken with a moan of delight. "I am so glad you came this weekend. Did you have fun?"

"It was a blast. Why aren't you in more classes though?" I uncork the bottle of wine I grabbed and fill up her glass.

"I can't enter most of them. I'm not considered a non-pro, because I help train horses for the ranch and have coached riders before. And I've earned too much prize money to be in the limited open. They all have their own sets of guidelines and I ride in the categories that I can." She takes another bite, devouring the food on her plate.

Clearing our dishes, I top up her wine and join her back at the table. "When is your next show?"

"Not until the end of July. I ride in the Spring Classic, the Summer Classic, and the Fall Classic; all out of that barn. It's my favorite venue, and it's close to home so that way my family never misses a show." She finishes her wine, waving me off when I try to fill it again.

Standing from the table, I clean up before taking her hand and leading her upstairs to her room. Lifting her shirt over her head, I rub my hands over her shoulders until she relaxes into my touch. She's been tense all day, all weekend, and I want to make her feel better.

The rest of her clothes fall into the pile before I strip down and lay her onto her back. Bracing myself over her, I kiss her softly. I want to savor the way she tastes and feels.

She wraps her legs around my waist, pulling me into her. Propping myself on my elbows, I slide in and out of her slowly, in no rush for this to end.

Her eyes are hooded as she watches me, flashing with emotions as we move together. We've never been slow together, and I don't want to be anything else with her right now.

Her arms wrap around my neck, her fingers playing with the hair at the base of my skull as we move together. Her body begins to tighten, her orgasm slowly building until she's crying out. "God, Alex."

My release follows, no less intense despite the quietness with which it comes.

Pulling out of her, I pull her back into my chest as she falls asleep in a post-orgasmic bliss.

I can't sleep. That wasn't just having sex, or making love, it felt like a goodbye.

Things with Lia are getting weird. It's been two nights, two nights since I didn't sleep a wink because all I could think about was feeling the end coming with Lia. I knew this would happen, what I didn't expect was my unwillingness to let her go.

We've spent time together over the past couple of days, but neither of us have addressed the elephant in the room.

Crossing the yard to Emma's, I let myself in and join her and Dane in their living room. Dropping into a chair with a sigh, I turn my attention to the show they're watching. The TV turns black.

"Okay, what's going on?" Emma holds the remote in her

hand. It's still pointed at the television, but she's staring me down.

"I don't want to talk about it." Slouching down in the chair, I'm sure I look like a petulant teenager.

"Is it the same thing Lia doesn't want to talk about? When she was riding some horses for me this afternoon she was unusually sullen." Dane smirks at the look on my face. "Don't look so surprised. You two aren't subtle at all."

"We're fine." My phone rings, and I'm relieved to be saved by the bell.

My relief is short-lived when I see who is calling. *Dad?*

Sending it straight to voicemail, I look back over at Emma and Dane. She's curled into him, his hand stroking her arm. For the first time since they've been together, I begrudge them their happiness.

"Alex . . ." My phone dings, letting me know I have a voicemail. Emma sighs. "Why don't you deal with whatever that is?"

Glaring at her, I finally pick up my phone when she crosses her arms, looking at me pointedly. I'm not going to win this battle.

Calling my voicemail, I listen to the message, and feel the blood drain from my face. Emma and Dane lean forward in concern, so I replay it on speaker.

*"Hi Alex, it's . . . Dad. Please call me, it's about your mother. I . . . Well, please call."*

Emma's eyes widen as he rattles off his phone number.

Standing, I stalk to the fridge and grab three beers. I hand two over to them before sitting back in the chair I've vacated, popping the cap on my own.

"Are you going to call him back?" Her words are cautious, knowing how touchy this subject is for me.

"Why? I haven't heard from him in more than ten years. He disappeared off the face of the planet and left me with a substance abusing psycho. What could he possibly have to say about her that I don't already know?" Tilting my beer back, I down it.

"I get what you're saying, I really do. The thing is, you haven't heard from him in all this time, so he's probably calling for a reason." Emma stands and comes over to sit on the arm of the chair, resting her hand on my arm.

"I know." Listening to the message again, I hear the concerned tone of his voice. Sighing, I tap his name before I can second-guess this decision. I could care less about whatever he has to say about most things, but Emma is right, I should hear it if it's about my mother.

"Alex, thank you for calling me back." My dad's voice sounds relieved, the noise in the background loud, making it difficult to hear him.

Ignoring any pleasantries, I cut straight to the point. "What happened to Mom?"

"She overdosed and is in the ICU. I'm here now, the prognosis isn't good and I thought you might want to come see her." His voice is matter of fact and I'm enraged that he can be so casual about her drug addiction, especially since he left me to deal with it.

"Yeah, okay. Can you text me the hospital and her room number? I will be on the earliest flight."

"Yeah, of course. Hey . . . I was wondering . . ." The noise quiets and I hear a door shut. Now I know he is in the hospital.

"I have to go. I guess I will see you soon, we can talk when I get there." Hanging up, I pocket my phone and pull Emma in for a hug. I'm rattled, part of me had wondered what happened to Mom, if she had ever cleaned up like she had been telling me. She had eventually quit texting, and I had hoped maybe she just gave up. I guess I have my answer.

"Hey, guys." Lia strolls into the kitchen, halting when she sees the look on our faces. I want to pull her into my arms, feel the comfort of her warmth, but I don't. "What's going on?"

Emma removes herself from my arms, grabbing Lia a beer from the fridge while I fill her in. "My dad just called. I guess my mom overdosed and is in the ICU. It doesn't look good."

My phone dings with the address of the hospital. Lia comes over, squeezing my shoulder as Emma hands me her laptop. I'm in a daze as I book my flight.

"Do you want me to come with you?" Emma offers, her voice soft.

"No, I don't want anyone to have to deal with this shit. I don't plan on staying long. All I need is a ride to the airport, I leave at noon, so we have to leave bright and early." Closing the computer, I hand it back to Emma, before reaching up to rest my hand on Lia's.

"I can drive you." Lia offers.

Nodding, I release her hand and stand. "I guess I better go pack."

We've been on the road for an hour, the silence surrounding us is not the comfortable quiet that Lia and I typically have. It's my fault, I know it is. She wants more than I can give her, and I don't doubt I've been sending mixed signals, but I've never been so conflicted in my life.

"We need to talk." I look over at her. It's possibly the worst time to have this conversation, but at the same time it's the best time since we will have a few days apart. I'm worried she's going to cry, and I hate the idea of hurting her, but we can't continue on anymore, not without progressing further into a real relationship.

"You're right. There is a lot that needs to be said, and while it's not the best time, we can't keep putting it off anymore." Her voice is soft. When she looks over at me, I can see how much she loves me. Before I can tell her I can't be with her anymore, she continues to speak. I brace myself for her to ask something of me that I can't give her. "I think we need to end our agreement."

She looks away from me, but she can't hide the sheen she blinks from her eyes. My jaw works as I process what she's said. It's the opposite of what I thought she was going to say. I thought she would try to convince me to try, but the easiness with which she spoke means she's been thinking this for a while, and the words cut in a way I didn't expect.

"You're right." I have to force the words out. *Why is this so hard? She's made it easy. No crying, no begging, just easy and simple. Exactly what we agreed.*

So why am not I not more thrilled?

"It's the best thing for our friendship." Her hands are white-knuckling the steering wheel, the only outward sign she's not as at ease with this decision as her voice would suggest. "We agreed we wouldn't continue on if it got to the point we couldn't maintain that, and I think we're there. I value your friendship too much to sacrifice it."

Nodding, my throat closes up and I can't think of what to say. I sink into the passenger seat as we fall silent again, the rest of the drive passes in a weird oxymoron of time. On the one hand, I don't feel we arrive at the airport fast enough, but as soon as she pulls up to the doors leading to departures, I'm not ready to say goodbye.

Lia gets out of the car, wrapping me in a hug. "Remember, they can't hurt you anymore. Family isn't always the family you're born into, sometimes it's the people you choose for yourself."

She steps away, her smile encouraging as I turn to leave. The knot in my stomach twists even tighter as I turn back only to see she is already gone.

# CHAPTER THIRTEEN

*Lia*

I arrive home mid-afternoon, exhausted from driving since six this morning. I wasn't surprised that Alex brought up our relationship, in fact Emma even warned me last night that he would probably pull away. I didn't need the warning, but I appreciate her concern.

She was pretty shocked when I told her I wasn't going to fight him on it. I know that I can't fight him for us, he needs to figure it out on his own, in his own time. I just hope he does, because my heart already hurts, and I feel nauseous at the idea of losing him for good. I want it all with him, not just friendship.

Mom and Dad are sitting on Emma's porch chatting with her and Dane when I get home. They wave at me, gesturing for me to join them, so I walk over instead of heading to the barn like I had planned.

"Hi, Sweetheart. We were just discussing Emma and

Dane's wedding." Mom stands, wrapping me into a hug that I sink right into. God, I love her hugs. It doesn't matter that I'm twenty-four, I could be fifty-four and still need her to hug me.

"You know I love wedding talk." Smiling as she releases me, I take an empty mug off the table and pour myself a cup of coffee from the steaming carafe. "I think all that's left to decide is the date, unless something else came up."

"That's what we were talking about. I want to wait until your show season is done, which is September, and then have a couple months to get everything in order. So we decided on November eighth." Emma's smile is contagious, and I return it with the first real smile I've had all day.

"That's perfect."

My phone erupts with several notifications at once, so I pull it out of my back pocket and scroll through them. Texts from Nella and Alex, an email from a new client, and another email from Lydia.

I start with Lydia. She hasn't been here to see Patty since she dropped her off, but I left her a message knowing how she's doing. Scanning over her email, she explains that her grandfather has been in the hospital, but he's being released and she wants to come see Patty. I write a quick reply, suggesting she come early next week. I don't have time for her this week, and I don't typically allow clients to come on the weekends.

Moving on, I read through the email from the new client and forward him my information packet, along with the consent form.

I leave Alex's text until last, confirming the schedule Nella sent me works.

Alex: Just checked into the hotel. Heading to
the hospital as soon as I drop my bags off in
my room.

Me: I'm glad you made it okay.

Three little dots show up, and I wait for him to respond. I didn't ask him to text me when he got there. Shaking my head, I fight the surge of hope. One text doesn't mean anything.

The dots disappear and then start up again. Setting my phone down, I pick up my coffee and tune back into my surroundings.

"We were really proud of you this weekend, Baby Girl." Dad smiles at me. He's started to get a little gray at his temples, and I think it makes him look distinguished. My brothers inherited their good looks from him. They share the same jawline and smile. The lady killer smile. "And not because you won, although you did kick ass. I think it takes real sportsmanship to encourage your fellow competitors the way you do."

"Thank you, Papa."

Conversation surges around me as Dad and Dane start talking about all the horses present at the show that Dane had trained. Several of which were offspring of some of our Quarter Horses.

Alex: Just got to the hospital. Dad is nowhere
to be seen, Mom is in ICU. Turning my
phone off.

"Alex arrived safely. He's at the hospital now." I turn to Emma, who holds up her phone.

"He just texted." She looks at me and I can tell she wants to say something, but is refraining because my parents are here. I know what she wants to say, so I just nod. She's reminding me to be patient. She's also giving me a pointed look that says I shouldn't take the fact that he thought to text me lightly.

He may not be fully aware of what he wants, but it's there. The question is, will he allow himself to fall, or will his fear at opening up his heart at the risk of getting hurt hold him back.

And how long am I willing to wait?

Nella plops down onto the arm chair. We're both covered in a layer of dirt from putting in a solid eight hours of work.

"It's a good thing my friend Andie got me into going to the gym. No wonder you're as fit as you are." She chugs water from the bottle I hand to her. "I signed up for an online course for July and August. I wanted to get it out of the way, and doing it online means it won't interfere with coming here."

Dropping down in the chair across from her, I wipe my face with a damp cloth. "What course?"

"Ethics in Psychology. The professor sent out an email today. He's partnering us up with another student for a research paper. We each write our own paper, but we share sources. Thank goodness, it means I only need to connect with them over the course chat that's been set up for us." She empties her water bottle, tossing it into the recycle bin I have across the room.

"Nice shot." I watch it fall in before looking back at Nella. This is only the second time she's been here, and she's already relaxing around me. She's still quiet, thinking through her words carefully. She doesn't say much, but when she does her words carry meaning. Nothing she says is for the sake of talking.

Smiling, I realize that I'm the complete opposite. I love to talk, especially once I've been drinking.

"It's late, would you like to stay for dinner before heading back to campus?" She lights up, nodding gratefully. "Great. I will text my brother and let him know to add another setting."

Ryan's builder finally broke ground on his house today, so Nella met him earlier when he came into the clinic swearing like the rough cowboy he is. As soon as he saw her, he immediately apologized and backed out of the clinic before she could even respond.

"The angry one?" She giggles. I don't think she giggles like that often because she smacks her hand over her mouth. "God, that sounded silly."

"He's just stressed because the crew was late today, and they were supposed to break ground last week. Plus, he's a control freak and the fact that the contractor kicked him out of the job site was a tough pill to swallow." I grab my keys from the desk drawer, locking up as we leave.

Nella follows me the short drive home. When she hops out of her car, her eyes widen as she takes in the two houses, medium indoor riding arena, the barn, and the fact that not only is Ryan having dinner with us but Emma and Dane as well. They're all sitting on the porch, watching us with interest.

"They're all harmless. I promise."

~

*Alex*

.  .  .

I'm ready to go home. I've been sitting beside a comatose mother for twenty-four hours, making civil conversation with a man I've hated since he walked out the door.

Closing my eyes, I picture myself back home. Seeing Lia's brown eyes smile at me over breakfast, or when we run into each other in the hall. Riding Chandler around the many miles of trails. I haven't even explored them all yet.

Lia and Emma have texted several times throughout the day to see how I'm doing. Their words of encouragement are the only things getting me through this. Especially since I know Dad wants to take me to dinner this evening and talk about whatever it is he feels he needs to say.

Opening the most recent text from Lia, I grin at the picture of Leo in a tiny saddle. He's on the lunge line, Lia in the center focusing on him. Nella must have taken the photo while she was there today.

Lia and I have been working Leo together four days a week since she gave him to me. And seeing her with him now makes me realize what a special person she is. She's actually continuing to be my friend, as we had agreed.

The entire flight I worked through a plan to make our lives easier. I didn't think the transition would be easy, but she's always said she's different than other women I've been with. And she's right. She's completely different.

This morning, the first thing I thought about was Lia. Texting her, wishing she was here. All day, I've wanted her by my side holding my hand as I wait for Mom to come out of the coma. I may deny myself a lot of things, but there is no denying I miss her or that I've let her in more than I ever intended.

There is even a part of me that is falling for her, I realize it now, but the other part of me refuses to let myself love her in that way. When you love someone, and give them your life, you hand over the power to tear you apart.

I've had enough people in my life who were supposed to love me and keep me safe tear away at me. I don't need to open myself up to another, not when I have the choice.

"Alex." My dad pops his head into the room. "Are you ready for dinner?"

Standing with a sigh, I look down at my mother. She's hasn't moved since I arrived, despite her vitals stabilizing. The doctor said that she was found within the small window of time where she can be saved. They're not sure about long-term effects, but they're hopeful she will make a full recovery, pending her willingness to finally sober up.

"Yeah. Let's get this over with." I follow him out the door.

We walk a block down the street to a quiet pub, sliding into a vacant booth. It's after the lunch rush and before the after work crowd starts to file in.

We order from the server, a woman in a skirt that barely covers her ass. I don't bother looking at the menu, just ordering whatever is on special.

Dad folds the menu. "Actually, two of those please."

She saunters away, probably hoping to increase her tip, but neither of us are watching her. Instead, I'm glued to watching my father tear a napkin into shreds. I may not have any clue as to who he is anymore, but I never remember him being nervous or avoidant.

"So, how's the family?" Leaning back, I cross my arms over my chest.

He flinches, before clearing his throat. "Good. Thanks for asking."

Tired of this awkward exchange, I dive in head first. "Let's just focus on why you're here. I'm sure the new Mrs. O' Neill isn't fond of you being here with you ex-wife and estranged son. So tell me what it is you want, and you can get on back home."

"I came because your mom never removed me as her primary contact, but mostly because I thought you would be here and there are things that need to be said."

"After all this time? You think now is going to make any difference?" I don't bother to lessen the hostility in my voice.

He sighs, leaning forward, and for the first time I can see honest regret in his eyes. "I never meant to hurt you, or your mother. Nor did I think she would fall off the wagon like she did. Shortly after you were born, your mom struggled with depression and turned to prescription pills. She got help, and had been sober for almost a decade.

"We had troubles in our marriage from early on. You were born before we got married, you know that, and we tried to make it work for your sake. However, when you were twelve something happened that year that changed everything."

He pauses, watching as I process what he's saying. "Obviously, I'm missing something. I don't remember anything happening that year."

"I guess it wouldn't stand out as an event that would impact your mother and me, but that was the year the Hayles moved next door."

Frowning, I wait as the server drops our food and drinks off. "I don't see why that would change anything."

"I don't know if you're aware, but Ben and your mother knew each other in college." He takes a hefty drink of his beer, expecting me to have a reaction.

"Actually, I did know. Emma found a photo of them. It was dated a few months before he met her mom." I bite into my burger, watching my father. "I don't see why that matters."

"I remember that photo, I was supposed to be there that night, but we had gotten into a fight." He doesn't touch his food, and mine is settling into my gut like a paperweight. "Your mom had a one-night stand that night. She was angry with me, had a little too much to drink and went home—with Ben. Things changed that night for us in every way. I loved your mom, but I couldn't forgive her for doing that."

"Rich, considering you met your new wife while still married."

"I'm not proud of that. There is more. A month later she found out she was pregnant. At first she'd hoped I wouldn't figure it out, but I'm good at math and I knew there was a good chance you were conceived that night.

"Alex, when the Hayles moved in next door, I couldn't handle it because it was a constant reminder of that night. When I saw him, and then looked at you, I knew I was right." He spreads his hands out in front of him, stumbling over his words, but I know what he's implying.

"Are you telling me Ben Hayle is my father? The man who stepped in to raise me when I was fourteen, was actually my birth father." The words are choked out, and I'm in complete disbelief.

"I had a paternity test done that year, before I left. It was negative, and your mother had only been with the two of us. Before I left, I told your mother to tell you and to tell Ben. I knew it was essentially hopeless, but I had to try. I think you deserve to know where you come from, and I want to apologize for not telling you. And for not being the father you believed I was. I never should have left you with your mother, I knew she was fragile, I just never expected . . ."

I slide out of the booth, cutting him off. "Enough. I need to go."

He calls after me, but I ignore him as I race out of the pub and hail a cab. Before I even know what's happening, I rattle off an address.

Ben Hayle is my dad. Emma is my half-sister.

Pulling out the photo I have of the four of us, I look

between us. Same height. Same build. Same eyes. Same brown shade of hair. *Holy fuck. I wasn't imagining it.*

The cab arrives and I toss him some cash before I'm out the door, winding my way through the plots until I reach the one I'm looking for.

**BEN HAYLE.**
**LOVING HUSBAND, DEVOTED FATHER.**

I don't say anything, I just sit on the ground and stare.

I have to tell Emma. How is she going to react to this?

Dropping my head into my hands, I breathe in a shaky breath. My lungs struggle, my heart pounds, and the base of my neck drips with sweat. My world is imploding, everything I thought about my life takes on new meaning.

*What does this really change though?* Emma and I already look at each other like siblings. Ben treated me like a son, without even knowing it was true.

Lia's words echo in my head. *Sometimes family is the people you choose yourself.*

I sit in the graveyard, dazed. Emotions flood my system at a rate that makes it hard to process it all.

How could she not tell me?

*This changes everything.* It seems odd that one piece of information could change my world, but it does. It doesn't begin to make sense, but something settles inside of me that always felt out of sync.

Dad: Your mom is awake.

Standing, I run my hand over the two headstones, side by side. I always considered them my parents in every sense of the word except biological. They were there for everything, my mom never even tried to fight them in order to get me back, I think she knew it was hopeless.

The cabbie is still in the parking lot, smoking a cigarette as he leans against the car. When he's done, I ask him to take me back to the hospital.

The short ride back is a numb blur. I'm in shock, and everything I've been avoiding my entire life has been let loose. Every excuse I've ever made for keeping people at arm's length, every reason for believing I had everything I need, all mock me.

My mind mocks me. My heart mocks me. More than half of my life has been made up of excuses. Excuses not to let anyone in. Excuses not to trust myself not to make the same mistakes my parents did.

Excuses, excuses, excuses.

Closing my eyes once I'm outside my mom's hospital room, I breathe in and try to settle myself before I go in there. The anger I've always felt towards them is miraculously gone, in its place is a sense of resignation.

Two sets of eyes look at me when I let myself into Mom's room. I can see tear tracks on Mom's cheeks, and instinctually know she knows I know.

"Alex, I'm sorry." Her voice is hoarse, but I shake off her apology.

"I don't want to talk about it." Sitting in the chair opposite Dad, I look at her with less compassion than I probably should, considering what she's gone through. "Listen, I'm glad you're okay. And I hope this serves as the wake-up call you need. Maybe I should wait until you're a little better, but I want to go home, so here it is.

"Don't contact me again, unless you've gone through at least six months of rehab, and six months of addiction counselling. That means, in one year, if you've figured out how to be a functioning person without the use of substances, you can then pick up the phone and call me. If you cannot accomplish this, I don't want to hear from you."

She starts to cry softly, but I've finally had enough of the lies and the manipulation. I want to go back to a life I've created for myself that's damn good. A life I built without them, hell, in spite of them.

I don't want to address him, but I do. He didn't handle things the way he should have when I was a child, he knows it. I can see the regret in his eyes as I stare straight into them. It's too late. Maybe I'm unreasonable, but I cannot forgive him for walking out of my life for something I had no hand in.

"I don't want to hear from you again."

Standing, I turn away from them and walk out the door without looking back.

# CHAPTER FOURTEEN



A knock on my bedroom door rouses me from a deep sleep. For the first night in a while it was dreamless. I've been so tired lately, it's no wonder I crashed.

"Lia? Are you all right?" Ryan pokes him head in, concern lining his face.

"Fine. Why?" Sitting up, I rub my eyes to clear the blurriness.

"Well, it's eight in the morning, breakfast time, and you're still asleep. You've been up and working at six every morning since you were nine." He leans against the doorway, watching my brain catch up to what he's saying.

"It's eight?" Grabbing my phone off the nightstand, I gape when I see he's not teasing me. "Holy shit. I can't believe I slept so long. I was exhausted last night so I went to bed at eight. I just slept for twelve hours!" Leaping out of bed, Ryan turns away as I scramble to change into clean clothes.

"Hence the worry. Emma made breakfast, we're waiting for you." He reaches behind him, shutting the door so I can finish getting ready for the day in peace.

My stomach grumbles as I sit at the kitchen table. "Sorry, I must be fighting a cold or something."

Emma hands me a plate loaded with fruit, scrambled eggs, turkey bacon, and hash browns. "Are you feeling okay now?"

Nodding, I cover a yawn. "Yeah, I feel fine. Still a little tired which makes no sense, but other than that nothing out of the ordinary."

As I eat, I find my energy and I race out from breakfast to fit a ride with Ollie in before I head to the clinic and deal with the mound of paperwork. The day passes in a blur, until I finally finish the last of my work.

Despite sleeping in, I yawn. Sitting in the office for most of the day was exhausting. It's something I avoid, which is why it took me the majority of the day.

Glancing at my phone to check the time, I am shocked to see I have a text from Dom.

Dominic: Hey… Could use a friend, can we meet at Linger tonight?

Mentally calculating how much time I need to get ready, I type a quick response.

Me: See you at 7. Let's eat while we're there, I'm starving.

Dominic: Thanks, Lia.

Racing home, I shower and change into jean shorts and a flowy tank top. It's as dressy as I will get aside from the occasional dress.

"Where are you going in such a hurry?" Emma peeks her head out of the kitchen. Walking in, I notice Dane and Ryan are cooking.

"I'm meeting Dominic for dinner. I have to be at Linger in twenty, I'll text you later."

Taking a huge bite of the burger set before me, my eyes cross at the burst of flavors. "This is my favorite burger."

Dom watches me in amusement, before cutting into his steak.

"So, what's going on? I don't think you've ever texted me to meet up once in the six years I've known you." Sipping my water, I dip a sweet potato fry in Linger's amazing dill dip.

He chuckles, shaking his head as he watches me devour another bite of burger. "Somehow, I always forget how direct you can be." Pausing as I moan and take another big bite. "Do you want me to leave you alone with that burger?"

"Dude, it has an onion ring on it. And Monterey Jack cheese. My mouth has never been as happy as it is when it's eating this." He smirks as I talk with my mouth full, shaking his head as he sets his fork and knife down.

"I had to put Wexle down today." Pain flashes across his face, and I finally understand why he needed me.

"Shit. I'm so sorry." Reaching across the table, I take his hand in mine. "What happened?"

"Colic. We didn't catch it in time. That horse was my world. He was the only consistency in my life, and now I don't have him anymore." He draws his hand away from mine, taking a deep drink of his water. We both decided to skip consuming any liquor tonight.

"Dom, you know you're never alone. I'm glad you reached out to me." My heart aches for him. Wexle was Dom's Ollie, and I can't imagine not having my boy.

"I needed to get out of the house." He laughs ruefully. "I've never really wanted to have any connections before, but today it dawned on me how truly isolated I am. Aside from work contacts, you are the only person I have. Pretty pathetic, huh?"

"You're busy."

"Being busy is an excuse people make for things or people they don't want to find time for. You run a successful business, work Ollie every day, have a close family, and maintain meaningful friendships. I go to work, I ride, and I go home." He leans back in the booth.

"Then change something." I say it like it's simple, but I know how difficult it is to change our routines.

Dom insists on paying for dinner before walking me to my car and giving me a hug. "Thanks for being here for me."

"Anytime. Hey, come by my clinic on Wednesday. We can have lunch." He opens my door, agreeing.

The entire drive home I cry to myself. Grieving for a horse I didn't even know that well. When I get home, I go straight to the barn and hug Ollie, crying into his neck. He breathes out a heavy sigh, nuzzling my hip.

"Lia? What's wrong?" Dane rushes into Ollie's stall, confused when he sees nothing wrong with my horse. "What did Dom do to you?"

Turning away from Ollie, I lean on his flank and stare at Dane in exasperation, tears still running down my face. "Seriously? He didn't do anything. He had to put his horse, Wexle, down today and needed a friend. I know you've seen him flirt shamelessly, but you don't know the first thing about that guy. And I'm crying because I'm an emotional woman who is grieving for a friend, because I can't honestly understand what it feels like to be in his shoes."

Dane reaches out, taking my hand and pulling me in for a hug. "I'm sorry. You're right. What can I do?"

"I have a horse that was surrendered to me in lieu of paying the bill. She has some basic reining training, but you can help Dom by continuing her training. I'm giving her to him." Dane walks me out of the barn and to the house. Stopping inside the door, he smiles at me and pinches my chin.

"You're a pain in the ass sometimes, but I'm damn proud to have you for my sister."

Bolting out of bed, I race to the bathroom and lose the entire contents of my dinner. Fucking great, now I have the god damn flu. Perspiration beads on my forehead as I heave until there is nothing left. Sinking to the ground, I curl up on the bathmat too tired to go back to bed.

# CHAPTER FIFTEEN

*Alex*

"Where is Lia?" Hugging Emma back, I load my suitcase into the back of her truck.

"I'm happy to see you too, jackass." She grins at me as she hops into the driver's seat. "She has the flu and has been forbidden from leaving her bed for the rest of the day. Poor girl has nothing left in her system."

I feel guilty that the first emotion I feel is relief that she's not avoiding me, before I'm filled with concern. "I've known that woman for a year, and she hasn't gotten sick once."

"I know. Trust me though, she wanted to be here." She turns onto the highway, setting the cruise control on the truck as we settle in for a long drive. "How's your mom?"

"She's expected to make a full recovery. I told her not to contact me unless she's been sober for one year." Adjusting the temperature, I turn the vent toward me. Part of me is glad

Emma picked me up, I can't keep in what I found out. I just hope she takes it okay.

"Wow. I think that's a reasonable expectation. And what about your dad?" She glances at me before focusing back on the road.

Nodding, I tap my finger on my knee. I practiced this big speech on the plane, going over and over the words in my head, but now that I'm sitting with her none of it fits.

"Umm yeah." My finger moves faster until Emma reaches over stopping it. My chest feels tight. This is going to change her entire world and the way she views her dad. "He told me he's not my father. My mom had a one-night stand and got pregnant."

"Wow. Okay. I can't imagine that was easy to hear. Did they tell you who your dad is? Do you think he will want to meet you?" Emma squeezes my hand before letting go. She's the most supportive person I know.

"Yeah, I know who he is." Angling my body towards her, I blurt it out. "It's your dad."

Emma whips her head towards me, swerving slightly on the road before returning her focus. A frown creases between her brows as she opens her mouth to speak before closing it without saying a word. Her face has paled as her brain catches up to what I'm saying.

Rushing on, I continue, "Apparently that photo you found, well, that night my dad was supposed to be there but they got in a fight. It was before your dad met your mom. He and my mom had a one-night stand. Then nine months later there I was. Dad even had a paternity test done because the dates didn't really add up in his head."

I stop talking, smoothing my hands over my jeans as I let her think. The seconds turn into minutes, and I'm preparing myself for a freak out.

"Well, I always did think you two had an uncanny resemblance." I jump when she finally speaks, gaping at her when the words sink in. "What? Did you expect me to be mad? The only thing I'm pissed about is that no one bothered to tell my father. He always thought of you as a son. Big brother."

She reaches over again, taking my hand in hers and holding on.

Relief surges through me. Emma is the only person in this world that I've never doubted letting in. She's been there for me through every major event in my life, unwavering in providing the friend I needed at the time. It was her suggestion that I move in with them, talking to her parents for me without betraying my trust. She saved me.

"Wow. That was easy." She laughs at the relief in my voice, shaking her head.

"You make things more complicated than you need to. Remember, the excuse of your parents only goes so far. You've now spent more than half of your life in part of a healthy family. You're a grown ass man, who has handled adversity better than the example set for him."

She's right. She usually is. "I know. It's just easier to keep people out."

"Life is pretty boring if we always choose the easy path. It gets pretty lonely too, when we don't let people in." Emma glances at me. I don't need her to say the name, we both know she is discussing Lia and the end of our relationship, for lack of a better word.

Clearing my throat, I take the bait. "I didn't hear from Lia yesterday, was she sick too?"

"No, she slept in and then had a ton of paperwork to do at the clinic. Then she met Dom for dinner." Emma takes her hand back to take our exit.

Fisting my hands, I swallow the bile that rises in my throat.

She had dinner with *Dom* last night? I hate that guy. I know I'm not mistaken by what I saw when she looked at me, so how could she possibly be moving on so quickly?

"Yeah, his horse had to be put down. I talked with Lia a little in between the vomiting. I guess his parents abandoned him in the hospital when he was a newborn. They didn't have any information on family, so he went straight into the system. He was finally adopted by an older couple when he was like eight. That's where he got his passion for horses, but they have both passed away from cancer." She shrugs. "Lia is really the only person who checks in on him throughout the year. He works his ass off, but his job requires him to be out of town a lot so he's pretty much alone all the time."

Okay, hating him a little less now. "Wow. It puts things in perspective, doesn't it?"

"I promised myself, actually that's a lie, I promised Lia I wouldn't say anything. However, I saw the look on your face when you thought she was on a date with Dominic. I want you to think long and hard about your reaction and the words you just spoke."

We turn into the driveway, and based on the set of Emma's shoulders I can tell the conversation is over.

She drops me off in front of the house, wishing me a goodnight as I drag my suitcase away from the truck. Toeing off my shoes, I peek in the living room when I see the light is on. It's late for Ryan to be up, so I'm not surprised when I see Lia on the couch. She's asleep, her eReader on her lap.

Abandoning my suitcase by the front door, I walk over to the couch, clicking off the light and lifting her into my arms.

"Alex?" She doesn't bother opening her eyes, she just wraps her arms around my neck and cuddles into me. It doesn't escape my notice how natural it feels to have her in my arms, and how my nerves from seeing my parents settle just by having her close. "How did it go?"

"It was . . . enlightening. Why are you sleeping on the couch?" I kick open her door, and lay her down on her bed. Tucking her in, I sit down when she finally opens her eyes to look at me. She looks exhausted and pale.

"I felt bad that I couldn't pick you up, so I was waiting up for you." She curls onto her side, watching me.

"Emma said you're sick."

"Was sick," she cuts me off. "I could have driven to see you, but I wasn't given the choice."

Before I can respond, her eyes drift shut, her breathing evening out as she falls back asleep. I sit for a moment, watching her at peace. It contradicts the chaos inside of me. The things I learned in the past few days was eye opening. I didn't let myself focus on more than the immediate issues, but now that I'm home I need to think. About what Emma said, and about the feelings I've been pretending don't exist.

All of that can wait until tomorrow.

"Hold the phone. You're half-siblings?" No one is eating, Dane's question loud in the kitchen. In fact, everyone has set their cutlery down and is waiting to hear the story. So, I fill them in on what my dad told me. Emma passes the photo around, and by the end it's unanimous that I look exactly like Ben.

Emma takes after her mother more, with her green eyes and darker hair. Which is why when we stand next to each other you would have no clue we're related.

"This is huge, and amazing news!" Lia touches my arm smiling up at me, before turning to Emma. "It's like a story in one of your books. You should totally use that in one of your books!"

Laughing, I pick up my fork and start eating again. I was expecting a bigger deal to be made of the news, even though the Hyatts have all shown themselves to be easygoing and understanding of everything.

"Are you feeling better Lia? You look much better than yesterday." Dane stands to grab a fresh carton of orange juice.

"I do. It must have been a twenty-four hour bug. I refuse to believe the burger I had with Dom is the reason, because I won't give up ordering it." Lia pushes her plate away. She might be feeling better, but she ate half her usual breakfast, and part of me suspects she's just putting on a brave face for her brothers. "But since I know you're still worrying, I asked Nella to come and help me at the clinic today."

After breakfast is done and the kitchen is clean, I saddle Chandler and head out to explore some new trails. I'm meeting Lia in a few hours to work with Leo and I've given myself that much time to sort through my shit.

Breathing in the fresh air, I try to sort through the jumble in my head.

I think I need to be honest with myself for the first time in a long time. I'm in love with Lia, and that scares the shit out of me. It's amazing how fear makes us so capable of lying to ourselves.

I missed her when I was out of town. I wanted her with me, I wanted to talk with her, and fall asleep with her. We had moved past being simply friends with benefits a long time ago. I want to take her on dates, and do couples things with Emma and Dane.

I can't believe I was so far in denial that I missed all the signs. I know I'm not exactly the most trusting person, but I didn't realize that included myself.

The question is, can I do this? Can I give this a shot?

I've spent twelve years keeping people at a distance, never committing myself to anyone. Emma was the only exception to that, and that relationship is completely different than what I'm contemplating with Lia. She will expect a future. Marriage. Children. And she deserves all of that.

Am I capable of being everything she needs?

*Lia*

Alex brushes Leo, a look of pure adoration on his face. I showed him how well Leo stands when being tacked. I wasn't wrong, he's a fast and eager learner.

Then I taught Alex how to lunge him properly, working through any issues that may come up. By the end, I was watching and just giving corrections. I would love to have Alex train Leo every step of the way, with help.

We let Leo back into the pen with Hoover, watching them play for a while. I bought them a ball last week, and they love it.

"Want to grab dinner tonight?" Alex leans into me. Closing my eyes, I breathe in and for a moment allow myself to enjoy the close contact. Having him back has been tough. Pretending that I don't love him, and that we're just friends is taking more out of me than I thought, but I promised myself I could do this. Having him as a friend is better than nothing.

"Yeah, that sounds nice."

Two hours later, we're eating dinner and laughing when I tell him how Ryan had scared Nella.

"You should've seen how fast he hightailed it out of my

clinic. It was hilarious." I finish off my burger, downing the rest of my water before continuing. "Anyways, thankfully things seem to be flowing more smoothly, because he was downright moody that day."

My stomach starts turning, but I ignore it. I'm enjoying my time with Alex too much to let anything disrupt it. By the time we're ready to go, my lower back is killing me because I'm so tense. I don't even argue with him when he insists on paying the bill.

We arrive home in record time, lingering outside. He's been acting odd this evening, it's a new side to him, but he's almost nervous. I've never seen Alex nervous before. He's probably feeling the awkwardness in our new reality too, unsure how I'm going to behave.

"Want to walk for a bit?" The suggestion is quiet, hopeful.

"How about we lay on the deck and look at the stars?" I propose. The idea of walking while my lower back is acting like a herd of elephants are hosting a dance party on it is unappealing.

He takes my hand, causing my heart to jump, and we walk to the back of the house. Laying side by side, we gaze up at the canvas of twinkling stars. He still hasn't let go of my hand. Part of me wants to pull away, ask him not to do that because it's too confusing. The other part of me wants to hold on tighter and not let him go.

"Are you okay, Alex? You've been acting off all night." Turning my head, I watch him in the darkness. The moon bathes us in a white light, allowing me to see his features clearly. My hand still holds onto his, the latter urge winning for the moment.

"I'm better than I have been in a while." His eyes do look lighter, like a weight has been lifted.

My heart sinks. A hopeless feeling settling in my already tumultuous gut.

"I'm glad." I am glad. I'm happy he's finding a way to be happy, I just wish it was with me.

"I've been thinking though." He pauses, and the look in his eyes has me holding my breath. "I miss you."

He turns his head to look at me straight on, I know he loves me, but he's looking at me like he knows it too. I want to shake myself. I must be imagining it. Missing me doesn't necessarily mean he wants more than what we had before.

"I'm right here." The words come out in a whisper.

"I know, but it's just not the same. I miss us. I want us to be together." He lifts our hands and holds them to his chest. I can feel his heart beating.

"You mean, re-engage our agreement? I can't do that Alex. I–I want more." He holds my hand tighter, as though he's afraid I'm going to pull away. I don't think I could, even if I wanted to. Regardless of what I'm saying, I will hear him out, and consider taking what he's willing to give me.

He leans into me, whispering, "I want more too. I've wanted more for a while, I was just too scared to admit it. I've been so scared of you hurting me, it took us parting for me to realize I'm more at risk hurting myself by not pursuing this than I am of being hurt by you if we do. I want to date you. I want people to know we're together."

My heart pounds, my eyes welling as I realize he means it. To my horror, I start to cry. And not a few glistening tear drops down my cheek. Ugly, full body sobs. My body shakes with the force of my tears, and I can barely make Alex out in the blur.

"Baby? I hope those are happy tears." He pulls me into his chest, holding me as I cry and try to catch my breath.

"S-s-so happy." I finally stutter out, before pressing into

him as close as possible. I thrust one leg between his, tangling us together.

He chuckles. "Good. Can you stop crying now so I can kiss you?"

Nodding, I press my face into his chest until the tears finally stop. Alex lifts my chin, kissing my forehead, then each cheek, the tip of my nose, before finally letting our lips meet. Opening for him, I pour everything I've been feeling into the kiss.

It's not hard, or rushed, it's slow and passionate. It's a kiss that tells me we're both finally in the same place. Not only am I stitched whole again, but so is Alex.

# CHAPTER SIXTEEN

*Lia*

Alex frowns when I come down the stairs. "Is that what you're wearing?"

"Ouch. You sure know how to make a gal feel pretty." I quip.

"That's not what I meant." He scowls when he sees my smirk. "And you know it. Wear jeans and your boots, with a nice top. I want you to be comfortable."

"You know what would make this easier? If you would tell me what we're doing." Grinning, I enjoy teasing him. I'm excited that he wants to surprise me. He's taking the dating thing seriously, and not wasting any time.

He shakes his head, pointing up the stairs without saying another word. As I change, I can't help the smile on my face. Our first real date where everyone knows it's a date.

Laughing as I remember the look on everyone's faces was priceless when we walked into the kitchen this morning holding hands. Emma was elated. Dane happy because Emma is so happy. Ryan's concern, and Jesse's shock. He was the only one who had no clue what had been happening between us. That shocked the shit me, that Dane and Ryan hadn't told him.

Overall, they were supportive, once my brothers had their fun warning Alex. Rolling my eyes, I throw on a deep green halter top. It showcases my breasts, but is comfortable to wear for whatever it is Alex has planned.

Bounding back down the steps, I spin in a circle at the bottom. "Better?"

"Wow." He pulls me into his arms, kissing me until we're both breathless. "We better go before I carry you upstairs, bend you over and—" a cough cuts him of.

"I'm going to pretend I didn't hear you saying that to my baby sister." Ryan is standing in the entrance of the kitchen, a sandwich in hand. Covering my smile as Alex shifts uncomfortably, I try not to burst into laughter.

Ryan is protective of me, but he trusts my judgment. It's kind of enjoyable watching him make Alex squirm though.

"Sorry, man."

Alex takes my hand and leads me out of the house. The laugh I'm holding in bursts free when Ryan winks at me.

Alex spins me, pressing me against the now closed door. "Think that's funny, do ya?"

Giggling, I nod. "Immensely."

He leans in and bites my neck before leading me down the steps.

"I don't know if Emma ever told you, but I've taken a bunch of photography classes, and done some freelance work. I thought today we could do a shoot with you and Ollie." He leads me into the barn where Emma has Ollie bathed, groomed, and looking show ready. "I got to thinking about what happened to your friend's horse, and I know you have photos from the shows you've been in, but . . ."

He fades off, waiting to see what I think. "That is the most thoughtful idea." Spinning around, I wrap my arms around him squeezing. "Thank you."

"Where do you want to start?" Alex asks as Emma hands him a professional looking camera, and a bag I'm assuming is full of different lenses. She smiles at us and leaves the barn without a word.

I run over all the places that would be nice to take photos, picturing the different spots in my mind. "Hmmm. Let's just go to the empty paddock outside. It's close, and the trees make a nice backdrop."

Alex takes my hand, my stomach fluttering at the contact. I want to tell him I love him, but I don't think he's ready for the words to be said. Regardless of whether I see the emotion in his eyes or not, he's already taken a huge step in taking our relationship to this level, and doing it well.

Opening the gate, we walk into the paddock and I wait while Alex gets his camera ready. He fiddles with buttons, changes the lens, and takes a few shots of me with Ollie while tweaking the settings.

"Okay, I don't want you to look at the camera. Just do some things with Ollie that you would normally do." He lifts the camera, and waits.

Laughing, I try to ignore him, talking softly to Ollie, and getting him to relax with me. He nuzzles my hip as I fix his mane, but I can't stop thinking about the click of the camera as Alex takes photos. Taking off his halter, I drop it to the ground. I don't want anything on him.

Moving to Ollie's side, I grip his mane, find my momentum, and swing myself onto his back. Smiling at Alex's muttered surprise, I lean down to stroke Ollie's neck, before nudging him into a trot.

I've been so focused on preparing for the shows that I haven't taken the time to ride Ollie bareback in months. I love the connection I feel with him, the movement of his muscles, and the absolute trust in him to take care of me.

I make a kissing noise and he seamlessly moves into an easy lope, moving off my leg perfectly. Bareback works the muscles of my entire body in a completely different way. There is no saddle helping me to keep my seat, it's entirely the feel of Ollie and using my muscles to move with him.

I angle across the paddock, changing directions, and circle around Alex. The camera he holds is no longer at the forefront of my mind, instead, I'm focused on Ollie and the enjoyment I always feel riding him.

Slowing Ollie down, I stop him and lie down on his neck, soaking up his warmth and the clean scent of his hair.

"Look over at me." Alex's voice is soft, the low timbre sending shivers down my spine. Pressing my cheek into Ollie's mane, I look over at Alex and await direction. He doesn't say anything else just snaps photos and moves around me. I can feel how relaxed my face is. I'm not smiling, but I know the look that's on my face. It's one of pure contentment.

I watch Alex move, the way his arms flex as he holds the camera. The intent focus on his face as he tweaks settings every so often. The heat that flares in his eyes when we make eye contact.

My body is humming, not wanting this date to be over, but ready to feel his body against mine as we move together. He lifts the camera. *Click.*

"I want you to lay on your back, with your head resting against his hip. Make sure your hands are comfortable, but not hanging limply." I can hear the lust in his throat, it settles into a steady flutter in my belly.

Last night, after we came inside, he kissed me outside my room before going to his bedroom and closing the door. I know he wants to show me that this isn't just about sex anymore, but I've known that for a while. As frustrated as I am, I think he needs to know that for himself rather than for me.

I just hope he doesn't plan on abstaining for long.

An hour later, we leave Ollie in the pasture to eat and make our way back to the house.

"I can't wait to see the photos. Can we upload them now?" Wrapping my arm around Alex's waist, I lean into him. I love the fact that I can do this without worrying about either of us overthinking it.

"Nope. You're not seeing them until I've gone through them all and picked out the best ones." He chuckles when I look up at him with a pout. "Do you believe that's going to work?"

"It was worth a try." Smiling up at him, I move in front of him and stand on my toes. He leans down to brush his lips against mine, deepening the kiss when I moan. I'm so incredibly turned on just being near him, I can't help the sounds that rumble from my throat.

A throat clearing has me reluctantly pulling away, only to be met with Dane and Emma watching us with a mixture of amusement and concern. We're on a roll today with the audiences.

It's obvious Dane is worried that Alex is going to hurt me. He knows how hurt I was after Graham, and I now realize I was never in love with Graham. Looking at Dane, I know he realizes my feelings for Alex are much stronger, which gives him the power to hurt me even more than I was.

I want to tell Dane not to worry, that I know Alex won't

hurt me, but there is no sense. It won't stop him, and he won't believe me when I tell him I can feel it. I'm not saying I am foolish enough to think we won't have issues, but I do think we can handle whatever comes our way.

"We're having a movie night and we thought you two might like to come over for our first official double date." Emma squeezes Dane's hand, and he finally relaxes a bit.

Looking at him, I mouth, "Trust me."

He nods. I love him for worrying, but I need him to understand I know what I'm doing.

"Sounds fun. We will see you later."

Emma: Don't eat dinner. We have food.

Me: Score! I was scrambling trying to think of what I want to eat. Nothing sounds good to me today.

Emma: I have lots of your favorites. So . . . How's it going with my big brother? ;)

Me: Why don't we have a girl's night soon and I can fill you in. You cook, I will bring the wine.

Emma: It's a date. See you later <3

Crossing the hall to Alex's room, I open the door and peer inside. It's empty, but I can hear the shower running in his bathroom.

When Mom and Dad built this house, they made sure all the bedrooms had their own bathrooms. I don't remember the old house, but Ryan does. It was a small, two bedroom house with one bathroom. After I was born, they knew they couldn't survive three teenagers and one bathroom, so they built this house. I'm definitely grateful for that forethought now.

Slipping out of my clothes, I step into the shower and press my chest to Alex's back. He turns to face me, grabs my wrists, and moves us to the back of the shower. A moan escapes my lips when he lifts my arms above my head with one hand, while trailing a finger between my breasts and down my stomach with the other.

"I knew I was in trouble as soon as you stopped fighting me." He presses his lips against my ear, his fingers pressing between my legs. "God, baby, you're so wet. You love it when I strip you of control."

Tilting my head back until it hits the shower wall, I moan out a yes as he slips two fingers inside of me. My body begging him for release.

He lowers my hands, pressing the palms to the walls. "Don't move them."

Dropping to his knees, he props one of my legs over his shoulder before swiping the tip of his tongue over my opening, circling my clit with the perfect amount of pressure. I can feel the vibration of his voice as he murmurs something against my pussy, before he presses his tongue inside me, kissing and biting me like a starved man.

My body is humming, the pressure building with the pleasure of his lips and tongue. Fisting my hands to fight the urge to tangle them in his hair and pull him closer, the leg I'm standing on shakes as my release hits, and if it wasn't for Alex's hands on my waist and his shoulder holding me up, I would be in a heap on the floor.

With gentle hands, he lowers my leg and kisses his way up my body until he's pressing light kisses along my jaw. "I missed your taste, and the way it feels when you come on my tongue."

Leaning forward, I kiss him hard, but before I can do anything else he is pulling away. "But . . ."

"We have to go to Emma and Dane's." He shuts the water off, his erection taunting me as he hands me a towel while laughing at my pout. "Later, baby. That's a promise."

Forty-five minutes later, we're in Emma and Dane's living room laughing at them as they bicker over what movie to watch. Rolling my eyes, I leave them to argue while filling my plate with snacks. Emma's deviled eggs catch my eyes. I love those things. Bee-lining it around the island, I pick one up when the smell hits me.

Dropping it, I glance over to the three of them and escape to the bathroom where I toss my cookies. *What the hell?*

Bracing myself on the seat of the toilet, I wait for the roiling in my stomach to pass while trying to figure out why I've been feeling so off. It's not until I'm standing in front of the mirror, making sure no one can tell I've just been sick when I'm slammed with the realization.

"Fuck. Me." Pressing my hand to my stomach, I stare at myself in horror as tears begin to fall.

"Lia, are you all right?" Emma knocks on the door. "You've been in there for a while."

Opening the door, I grab her arm and yank her into the bathroom. Her gasp as she takes in my appearance sounds muffled over the ringing in my ears. How could this happen? I take my pill every day at the same time. Alex is going to flip his shit, we had the conversation so many months ago in the kitchen, right before he fucked me into oblivion with that gorgeous cock.

"I–I think," fading off, I wipe my eyes and grip the counter.

Looking at Emma through the mirror, I finally whisper, "I think I'm pregnant."

Emma's mouth opens and closes a few times, she looks as stunned as I do, and I can't stop the laughter that bubbles up as I look at the both of us in the mirror. Bending over the counter, I laugh until I'm crying, and then I'm just sobbing uncontrollably.

"Shhh. It's going to be okay. You've always wanted kids." Her hands rub my back, soothing me.

"Em, I did. Well, I do. It's just—Alex." That one word stills her hand. His name is all I need to say, but we both know what I'm thinking.

He's just wrapped his head around the idea of dating me, of letting me in when his fear of being hurt has kept everyone at arm's length for over a decade. His willingness to try and do real couple things, doesn't equate to a willingness to be tied to me forever. And regardless of what happens between us, a child will tether us to each other, always.

Emma spins me to face her, wiping my face with a damp cloth I didn't even notice her wetting. "Lia, everything will work out. Go to the doctor, get yourself accustomed to the idea, and then tell him. Don't wait too long though, he needs to know."

"I know." Turning back to the mirror, I fix myself up as best I can, my hands shaking.

Emma opens the door, and we join our men in the living room.

# CHAPTER SEVENTEEN

*Alex*

Black shadows mar the usually creamy skin beneath Lia's eyes. She came back from the bathroom last night pale and tense, but when I asked what was wrong she just muttered that she wasn't feeling well.

Then when we got home, she fought me for control again, something she hasn't done in over a month. I feel like we've taken some steps backwards and I don't know why. This morning she was out of bed before I woke up, cooking break- fast. But then she asked if I wanted to come with her to show Dom the horse she wants to give him.

Now, I'm sitting on the fence as she rides the mare, showing him what she can do. Instead of the usual elation that's on her face when she does anything with horses, all I see is strain and worry.

Her usually vibrant smile, the one that lights up her face, is missing. Her voice lacks its usual enthusiasm. Everything about her is dulled, like she's lost her sparkle. Dom has picked up on it, but she just keeps repeating that she's tired today. I don't think she's lying about that, but everyone has commented that she's not herself.

Thinking back to breakfast, the look she and Emma shared keeps sticking out. Something is going on, and it's making me a paranoid wreck. Surprisingly, I'm not worried about Lia and me, I'm just worried about Lia. I've never seen her like this, and it would be like her to keep something from me to protect me.

I don't need her to protect me, I need to do that for her. It's my job to make her smile, and right now that's not happening.

"I can't believe you won't let me pay for her." Dom's voice cuts into my musing. He seems excited about the new horse, and the plans that Lia and Dane have for her, but Lia just looks exhausted and like her head is everywhere else.

"Dom, she was surrendered to me in lieu of payment. You're going to give her the perfect home, that's all I want." Lia dismounts and gives him a quick hug. They walk towards me, and for the first time all day, Lia's eyes match her smile.

His smile is all teeth as he rubs the mare's neck. "I was hoping I could board her here. I bought a small bit of acreage not too far from here, and I thought maybe you could coach me."

"You're moving close? You want me to coach you? What about your job?" Lia's mind is working a mile a minute, her words stumbling out so quickly, it's hard to follow.

"One at a time. I had a lot of savings from working out of town so much. I've always loved this area, and I found the perfect lot. Why wouldn't I want you to coach me? You're incredible. Lastly, I got laid off. I'm okay with it, I didn't love what I did. It's time to figure it out. The only good thing about my job was that it paid me a lot and made it so I can take some time to figure my shit out."

"Call Dane, he deals with boarding and what not. I don't think it should be an issue. He also might know of some work you can do." Lia links her fingers with mine, her hand gripping me tightly. When I look over at her, I notice she has paled.

"Thanks, Lia. I will call him. And the coaching?" Dom releases the mare from her halter before turning back to us. His eyes flick to me, and I can see he is concerned.

"Yeah. I can do that. I've avoided taking on clients to coach lately, but I will do it for you." She smiles, her posture relaxing again as though whatever was happening passed. Watching her carefully, my gut is going wild telling me something is up.

"You rock. Thanks, Lia! Well, I better head home. I have to start packing." Dom waves at us as he heads to his truck, a broad smile on his face.

"It looks like they're going to be a good fit." Lia steps into me, dropping my hand and wrapping her arms around my waist. Looking down at where her head rests on my chest, I watch as her eyes close as she breathes me in.

When her arms tighten, my heart starts to pound. She finally opens her eyes and gazes up at me. "I have a doctor's appointment this afternoon. I wanted to talk to him about why I've been feeling so off lately. Maybe we can go for a picnic tonight. Ride the horses to one of my favorite spots, and enjoy a quiet night. What do you think?"

Kissing her forehead, I push aside the worry. She's not feeling well, that's all this is. She's not pulling away from me for any reason other than that. "Sounds perfect. Why don't I get everything ready while you're at the doctor's office?"

Barging into Emma's kitchen, I startle her and Dane. "Something is going on with Lia, and I know you know what it is, Emma, so I'm going to need you to tell me."

Dane narrows his eyes and crosses his arms. I can tell he doesn't like my tone of voice, but he can piss off. Ignoring him, I stare down my sister, who is looking everywhere but at me.

"Look at me. Emma, she's acting distant and I need to know why." Dropping into a chair, I run my hands down my face. "I don't want to lose her. I finally have my own shit figured out, and now she's pulling away from me."

Emma's eyes snap to mine. *Finally.* What I see there confuses me. She looks worried, but happy. She's also shaking her head. "Alex, I love you. And I love Lia. She's not pulling away from you, she's just got a lot on her mind."

"Why can't she share it with me? I know I'm no expert, but isn't that what you do in a relationship?"

Dane is looking between us, confused. Obviously Emma hasn't told him what's going on. I don't know if that should worry me more or less.

"Lia loves you. She will tell you when she's ready." Emma's tone leaves no room for argument. Instead, she moves around the island and lifts a couple saddle bags. "Now, Lia told me you're going for a picnic. These will attach to Chandler's saddle."

Getting up, I take them from her, bending to kiss her cheek. We don't say a word as I walk out of the room, but before I leave the house, I can hear Dane asking what's going on. Resisting the urge to eavesdrop, I head to Lia's kitchen to prepare a romantic picnic, trying to ignore the frustration at not having any answers.

## *Lia*

"It looks like you're about six weeks along. I trust you've stopped taking your birth control pill?" Dr. Meyer looks up from the clipboard in his hands, his face expectant.

"I just realized last night that's probably why I've been feeling so off. I have been taking it until this morning." I'm white-knuckling the arms of the chairs. Six weeks? Okay, lots of time to adjust to the idea that I'm having a baby. With Alex. Whom I love, but who will probably freak the shit out as soon as I tell him. Actually, there is no probably about it. He will freak out. And, knowing him, he's going to need some time away from everything to adjust. That just stresses me out more.

"Perfect. I want you to start taking a pre-natal vitamin. Here is a list of some I would recommend." He hands me a post-it note. My first thought is that it seems weird a doctor would write that on a post-it and not something more official, but I guess since I don't need a prescription it makes sense that he wouldn't waste his time typing it out. "And here," he hands me a small photo, "is the sonogram."

I'm glued to the black and white photo. The small bean that will grow into a little person. "Thank you." The words are hoarse, and I don't look away from the picture of my baby.

"The receptionist has set up your next appointment. You can continue with your normal daily activities. It sounds like your symptoms are manageable, but if the nausea becomes too much call in and we can explore some medication to help." With that, he leaves me in the room, staring at a photo that changes my life.

I have to tell Alex. I have to tell my brothers. I don't know which scenario I'm more scared for. On the one hand, Alex is likely to shut down. But my brothers are likely to hold a shotgun to Alex's head and force him to marry me.

Okay, both are equally scary for different reasons.

> Emma: Alex came in here asking what's wrong. I didn't say anything. Now Dane is hounding me. I had to distract him with a blow job.

> Me: Ew, I didn't need to know that. Thank you for having my back.

> Emma: How did it go?

> Me: I'm six weeks along. Healthy. Now I just need to tell Alex.

> Emma: . . . yeah. If you need me, I'm around.

Sticking my phone in my pocket, I try not to let the tone of Emma's text scare me from doing this tonight. It's like ripping a Band-Aid off, the quicker the better.

By the time I've parked my car, my stomach is a flurry of butterflies. Not normal butterflies though, butterflies that have armored up and gone to battle. It feels great when my stomach has already been iffy today.

The door opens, and Alex bends down pressing me into the seat as his lips mold to mine. I can feel the tension in his body, the worry he is carrying that I'm going to be another person to hurt him. I hate that he feels that way, and I'm not sure he's wrong.

I don't doubt that once he grows accustomed to the idea that he will eventually warm up to it, what I worry about is the tie this creates. What if he realizes he doesn't want anything more but feels obligated to be with me?

I couldn't stand that. And he would too. He would make things work because he is loyal like that.

When he pulls away, I see the love and worry shining in his eyes. It's like a balm to my soul. No, this is just hormones. My mind is freaking out because I've had information overload in the past twenty-four hours.

Alex takes my hand, helping me out of the car. I snatch my open purse from him, zipping it shut with an apologetic smile. My pre-natal vitamins are in there, and I don't want him to see them. The sonogram is in my back pocket, ready to pull out whenever I work up the nerve.

"The horses are ready." He bypasses the awkward moment, taking my hand and leading me to the hitching post outside the barn.

We untie the horses, step up into our saddles, and start off into a trot.

The trail is beautiful in the low light of evening. Spots of light shine through the vibrant leaves on the trees. The spot I'm thinking of stopping at has a beautiful view of the mountains. It also allows us to ride side by side.

"How did your doctor's appointment go?" Alex breaks the silence, looking over at me. His hands are relaxed, holding the reins low on Chandler's neck.

Staring straight ahead, I chew on my lip. "He said that I'm healthy."

I'm not ready to tell him, although the ability to ride away quickly is appealing. I finally glance over at him so he can see I'm not lying.

He changes the subject, telling me about how he spent some time with Leo while I was at my appointment. Hearing him talk about his colt relaxes me, and by the time we reach our destination, the butterflies in my stomach have settled.

We tie our horses, before settling onto the blanket Alex packed with him. He brought croissants with turkey, onions, lettuce, and a light aioli sauce. There are also containers with nectarines, peaches, strawberries, cherries, and raspberries.

"This is amazing. Thank you."

We eat, chatting about some of the things we can add to Leo's training. It's easy being with Alex like this, and I find myself relaxing.

He tucks a strand of hair behind my ear, leaning in to brush a soft kiss on my lips. "You're amazing."

I take a bite from a strawberry, moaning when he leans in to kiss the juice from my lips. His hands wrap into my hair as he lays me down on the blanket, covering me with his body.

We slowly take our clothes off, taking our time to enjoy ourselves. I love how gentle he's being with me, but he knows what I crave. He pins my arms above my head, restraining me, as he quickens his pace, thrusting in and out of my pussy. Wrapping my legs around his waist, I feel the orgasm building.

"I fucking love how you feel. You love it when I hold you, restrain you." Alex groans, kissing my neck before devouring my lips.

My pussy clenches his cock, my release ripping through me with a cry. "God, yes. Alex."

His own orgasm follows, the warmth of his release filling me. Our connection has been strong from the moment we laid eyes on each other. I felt it grow deeper the moment my heart opened itself to him, and now that we're having a baby, the connection will be forever forged in a way I never knew was possible.

We're lying facing each other on the blanket, Alex's fingers playing with mine. I look into his eyes, memorizing this moment. A moment when he is looking at me in happiness and affection, a moment to hang onto because I know it's going to be gone as soon as I open my mouth.

"You look far too stuck in your head, considering the orgasm you just had." Alex teases me, his eyes sparkling.

Sighing, I drop my eyes to where our hands are joined, squeezing his tighter as though I can hold him here with me by that strength alone. "When I went to the doctor, he told me I was healthy, but he also told me something else."

Alex's brows come together.

Before he can speak, I forge on. "Alex, I–" taking a deep breath, "I'm pregnant."

His face pales, his Adam's apple bobbing as he swallows. "I . . . How? You're on the pill."

I watch him, fighting tears as his eyes shutter. I expected this, but it doesn't hurt any less. My voice comes out as a whisper. "I'm the exception to the rule."

He sits up, pulling his shirt over his head as he scrambles to get dressed. I follow, until we're both standing, facing each other.

I wait for him to turn away from me, but he pulls me into his arms, kissing the crown of my head. "I need some time to process this."

"I know."

The ride home is silent, and as soon as we've put the horses out to pasture he's gone.

# CHAPTER EIGHTEEN

*Alex*

I'm just driving. I don't know where I'm going. I don't know when I will stop. I need to stop. Instead, I head to the mountains. I find a campground, and I book a night.

*Pregnant.*

Rushing to the bushes, I throw up. My hands brace on my knees as I lose everything in my stomach, until I'm dry heaving.

I probably look deranged.

*Pregnant. I'm the exception to the rule.*

Holy shit. A baby. Someone to look after. Someone entirely dependent on *me.*

Grabbing a water bottle from my truck, I rinse my mouth out.

Dropping the tailgate to my truck, I grab the blanket I always keep in my backseat, lay it out, and settle in for a long night.

I doubt I will sleep. My mind is racing, barely holding off a panic attack as I think about what a baby is going to change. Lia is more than capable of handling this. That woman is incredible, and there is no doubt in my mind she will excel at parenthood.

I, on the other hand, have never even thought about children.

Until Lia, I didn't really think about anyone other than myself. Aside from Emma, but she's an exception. Like Lia.

She's been my exception, and now she defied another odd and got pregnant while on the pill.

Shit. Emma knows.

My mind whirls, a chaotic storm as I try to filter through the panic.

*A fucking baby.*

Lifting my knees, I lower my head and focus on breathing.

I need to calm down before I go home. Lia needs me to have my shit together.

*Lia.*

The look on her face when she told me. She was worried about how I would take it, but she knew I would need to get away. How long will she tolerate me getting my shit together though? I can't go back yet.

*I can't believe I ran.*

No, not run. I just need to clear my head. She understands. It's not like I didn't tell her I needed time. She knows me. She accepts me. She loves me.

My heart starts to slow. Thinking about Lia is helping me slow my brain. I just need to work through this. Then I need to go home and show her I can be there for her.

Once I wrap my head around the fact I'm going to be a father.

Holy fucking hell.

**Lia**

I'm in a foul mood when I wake up the next morning. I know I'm being irrational, and I knew Alex would likely leave so he could process alone, but the fact that he hasn't even contacted me to tell me he's safe pisses me off.

Storming into the kitchen, I startle Ryan and Emma who are already cooking.

"I thought you might like the morning off." Emma's voice is soft.

It's clear I'm barely holding myself together. It's also apparent that Alex didn't come home, since his truck is still gone.

I knew this would happen. So why am I so mad?

Oh right, pregnancy hormones.

"Thanks," I mumble. Emma stops me from grabbing a coffee, earning a glare. "Let me have a cup of coffee."

"No."

Ryan looks between us as he removes a waffle from the iron and pours in new batter. He's wisely not saying anything.

Emma moves to pour me a glass of juice, handing it to me silently.

"Did you hear from him?"

She shakes her head.

"So it's not just me then?"

Dane and Jesse file in as Ryan settles the plate of waffles onto the table. My mood is picked up on instantly.

"What's wrong with you this morning?" Dane elbows me gently as he moves past.

To my horror, I burst into tears. My anger fading into fear and sadness.

I need to get myself under control.

"Holy shit." Jesse stares at me wide-eyed. "Dude, what did you do?"

"I, err, I was just kidding." Dane tucks me into his side, his voice baffled.

"Okay. Everyone sit the fuck down. Lia, what's going on?" Ryan takes charge of the situation, his big brother voice leaving no room for argument. Part of me wants to pick a fight, just for the sake of arguing, but the rational side manages to win. Nodding, I sigh.

My brothers sit me between them, angling their chairs towards me.

Looking to Emma, she just waits. I know she's letting me decide what to do, and her silence is her way of supporting whatever decision I make, but I want her to push me.

"I went to the doctor yesterday. To see why I've been so tired and nauseous." Dane and Ryan both squeeze my hands tighter, worry lining their foreheads. "I'm pregnant."

Silence.

It's amazing how loud the quiet can seem when all you want is someone to say something.

"Okay," Ryan breathes out. I can tell he's trying to think of the words he needs without upsetting me. "I'm guessing Alex knows."

"He knows."

"Where the fuck is he?" Dane's voice is tight, his eyes flashing.

"He's processing. Which I knew he would need to do. We just decided to become official, and now this bomb is dropped. I'm still wrapping my head around it, and I expect that he's doing the same." Wrenching my hands from my brothers, I flex them for a moment before resting them on my stomach.

"He should be doing that here, with you."

Shaking my head, I defend him even though I wish that's what was happening. I woke up this morning not okay with him leaving. Is this what's going to happen every time something big comes up? Or will there ever come a time when he can talk to me about it?

I want him to talk to me. It's okay if he's not okay with this yet.

I can be okay for the both of us. How can I support him if he isn't here? How can I show him that we can handle this?

Jesse says something, and they move away to talk quietly amongst themselves. I don't hear the rest of the conversation.

I eat quickly, and excuse myself to go to the clinic and work.

Alex didn't come home again last night. He didn't text or call either. I've moved from the understanding I found yesterday, back into the zone of pissed off.

"Whoa. I know that look." Lydia walks into the clinic. Patty gets to go home today, and I forgot she moved her appointment from eleven to ten.

She closes the door behind her, and when I look up I see a shadow of the friend she once was. Not that I trust her anymore, but she once knew me better than anyone.

"It's been a rough few days." Standing, I slip my boots on and leave the clinic. Patty is ready to go, so I lead Lydia around the building to where she is grazing. "She responded well to the therapy. Ease her into riding. Start with some groundwork, move to short spurts, and build up her stamina again."

"Lia, I know I'm probably the last person you want to talk to, but I'm here if you need someone. Is it Alex?" Her voice is soft, compassionate, and all it does is add fuel to the fire burning inside of me.

"We're fucking fine." She steps back, her face paling. "Shit. That was unprofessional. I'm sorry, Lydia. It's the pregnancy hormones."

She gasps. "You're pregnant?"

"Yeah, I found out this week. Still adjusting to the news; it was a surprise. Anyways, I don't want to talk about it. I'm just tired."

We load Patty into the trailer. Lydia looks at me, her mouth opening and shutting a few times, before she thanks me and pulls away.

I don't even feel a pang when I think about what we used to have. It's amazing how I've let go of something I used as an excuse to isolate myself for so long. It's also fascinating to look back and recognize that while Lydia and I were friends, it's nothing compared to the friendship I have with Emma.

What Graham and I had is nothing compared to what Alex and I have found together.

Everything happens for a reason, and I need to hold onto hope that this is just opening the door for something great.

"Right, Little Bean? Everything is going to be great." Resting my hands on my stomach, I find peace with this new adventure.

I'm still pissed off at Alex, but I know he needs to find his peace too. And if he doesn't come around, I will hunt him down and force him to work through it with me.

# CHAPTER NINETEEN

*Lia*

Alex didn't come home again last night.

I broke down in Emma's arms, crying about how I'm going to lose him. She listened to me weep, and go on about why he won't love me anymore. Finally, she told me I was being ridiculous.

I woke up this morning feeling better. I slept well, I didn't throw up, and I don't have any clients today.

Leading Ollie into the arena, I swing onto his back and start warming him up. The summer reining show is at the end of the month, and I've upped my practice time.

In a few short months, my life has changed drastically. April brought about a change that I never expected to lead here. I guess it was time.

Once we've warmed up, I start working him.

We lope circles, practicing lead changes until they're perfect.

This is what I need. I love the way everything falls away when I'm with Ollie. The way my hair flows behind me, it's like every worry falls away from the tips of my hair.

All that's left is me, Ollie, and the rush of speed and a clear mind.

We move from lead changes to spins. Yesterday I felt too nauseous to ride, so Ryan rode Ollie for me. I stop him, relieved my stomach is cooperating with me today.

Ollie needs very little correction before his spins are perfect. Timing, feet movement, head position, everything is lined up the way it's supposed to be.

Trotting him to one end of the arena, I face the opposite wall and click him into a lope. We pick up speed until I kick my heels out, asking him to stop. His hind legs dig into the sand as his front legs move. The slide is perfect.

Turning him, we go again. And again. And again.

"What the fuck do you think you're doing?"

**Alex**

Lia wasn't in the house or at her clinic when I got home.

Now, I'm staring at her practicing sliding stops like she isn't carrying our child.

Crap, I can't leave her alone ever again.

She stops as I yell at her, trotting towards me.

"What?" Her voice is calm, making my eyebrows shoot up into my hairline.

Grabbing her waist, I haul her down. "That's too dangerous for you and the baby. What do you think you're doing?"

"Practicing for the show. That's what professionals do." She speaks to me slowly, like I'm an idiot.

"You're not doing the show. Not in your condition." I wave my hands in front of her stomach.

"My condition? Alex, I'm pregnant. I'm not a bomb waiting to go off."

"It's too dangerous. I don't want you riding like that."

Her eyes flash. I woke up this morning and realized that despite how terrified I am, the fact that I'm having a baby with Lia fills me with joy.

It took me a few nights to get there. Walking the fine line between joy and panic, but that's probably natural. If you go by the movies, anyways.

"You listen to me right now. The doctor said I can do everything I was doing before. I will ride in the show. I will practice like I always do. And there is nothing you can say that will stop me." She gets in my personal space, her head tilting back to stare at me. "Now, are you back for good? Or are you going to disappear without a word to anyone again?"

She's pissed.

Before I can say anything, she's turned back to Ollie and is lifting her foot into the stirrup. Wrapping my arms around her waist, I pull her back down. She is cursing at me, but I lift her into my arms and carry her out of the arena. Ollie follows behind us, into the barn.

Dane is inside, cleaning stalls.

"Dane, can you please take care of Ollie while I talk to your sister? Thanks." Without waiting for a reply, I continue out of the barn.

"You're behaving like a caveman." She wraps her arms around my neck and rests her cheek on my shoulder whispering, "I was worried."

Kissing the crown of her head, I carry her upstairs, into my room, and lay her on the bed. Crawling next to her, I pull her into my chest. "I'm sorry. I woke up this morning and realized I can't run away to process things like that. I need to talk it through with you."

She looks up at me, her eyes still upset. "I understand needing to take a walk, but disappearing for a few nights without a word isn't okay. I need to know you're not going to do this for every major thing that happens."

"I know. I'm sorry, baby." Kissing her gently, I pull back. "So, a baby. How are you feeling?"

"I'm okay. My symptoms come and go, but they've been manageable. I'm not dropping the shows."

"Yes, you are."

"No, I'm not. I already talked to my doctor about it the day I found out. He said I can ride. So I'm going to ride." She stares me down, unwavering in her resolve.

"We will see."

I'm determined for her not to put herself and the baby at risk. If I can, I'm going to convince her to ride for fun, but nothing more. I'm not an idiot, I know I can't keep her off horseback her entire pregnancy, but maybe I can keep her from doing anything that is high risk.

Lia rolls her eyes, reaching into her back pocket. She hands me a small photo, it's crinkled. Flipping it over, I see it's a sonogram. "There's our baby."

My gaze flicks between the sonogram and Lia. Her eyes are shining, and I know that she's excited about the baby. She got there on her own when I should have been there to support her.

"I promise, I will be here every step of the way. I won't disappear again. I shouldn't have done that. I didn't know I wasn't coming home until I pulled into the park. I'm sorry I wasn't here for you." Clutching the sonogram to my chest in one hand, I gently push Lia onto her back and rest the other on her stomach.

She watches my hand, all worry fading from her face as she finally smiles at me.

In that moment there is nothing more that I want than the whole package with her.

"Lia, will you marry me?" The words are out before I've consciously made the decision, but they feel right.

She jolts up, staring down at me in shock. "What? You're kidding, right?"

"No. I think we should get married before baby comes." I sit up too, running my hand through my hair, before taking her hand in mine.

She's staring at me, a mixture of emotions flashing across her face. I wait patiently for her to sort through her thoughts and answer.

"Alex, I–I can't. I'm sorry. You're only asking me because of the baby. We haven't even said 'I love you' to each other yet. We're not there yet." She pulls her hand away, taking the sonogram from the clutches of my hand and smoothing it out. "Let's just be us. It's enough for me."

Resting my hand against her cheek, I nod before kissing her. Her eyes close, her lips parting as I deepen the kiss. She pulls me back down onto the bed, her hands running over my body. I know she thinks I've accepted her answer.

I haven't.

# CHAPTER TWENTY

*Lia*

We told my parents last night. It went better than I thought it would. Once they got over the shock, they both were excited their first grandbaby is on its way.

Alex wraps his arms around me as I cook lunch. "Hey, baby."

He's been attentive and loving. I know he's trying to make up for disappearing by proving he is excited for baby and that he doesn't plan on going anywhere again. I forgave him as soon as I saw him, I just needed him to know it can't happen again.

We've argued every day over the horse show, he still thinks he can win that one, but every day I find time to practice. And every day he stands there and glowers at me.

"How was Leo this morning?" Turning in his arms, I kiss him before he can answer.

"Wonderful. He's learning everything so quickly. Dane is

really impressed, I think he's disappointed we gelded him. Says he would have made a good stud." Alex lifts me onto the counter, kissing my belly before taking over the cooking.

"We don't need any more studs around here."

Alex nods. He's been spending more time around the ranch, learning about the different areas. Specifically the training and breeding programs that Dane runs. He's still running his graphic design business, but he wants to be more involved on the ranch too, especially since my ability to help will be limited once my belly gets too big.

It's been a week since he came home, and once my brothers had a chat with Alex, they've embraced the pregnancy. They've all gone into protective mode, driving me crazy with their need to do everything.

No one will let me tack Ollie. I don't even have a bump yet, but they're treating me as though I'm going to pop any day now. It would be kind of cute if it wasn't so annoying.

"Ryan called, said he would be home for lunch. That was about twenty minutes ago. If you're hungry, I'm sure he won't mind if you start eating." Alex shuts off the stove, dishing up the stew I have been cooking all day.

The front door slams shut. Looking at Alex, I raise my brows as I hear Ryan cursing. A bunch of thuds and banging sounds through the house, until he pushes his way into the kitchen, his left arm cast in plaster and tucked in a sling.

"What the fuck happened?" Jumping off the counter, I ignore the glare Alex shoots me as he carries three bowls to the table.

"I got fucking kicked by this bastard of a horse. Actually, it's not the horse's fault. It's lack of communication on the part of the damn owner." He drops into a chair, and dives into eating his stew. "I called Dane already. Of course he started in on finding someone to come in and cover me. He wants me to take an apprentice because he thinks I should hire someone."

Ryan sneers. Dane and Ryan have been arguing over this for a couple of years. Ryan has always won, but knowing Dane, he's already got feelers out. I have to admit, I think Dane is right.

"Well . . ."

"Don't, Lia."

Sitting next to him, I rest my hand on his arm. "Ryan, at least think about it."

"Fine." The grumble is less severe considering he's got a mouthful of stew, so I grin at Alex and dig in.

"Open your eyes." Alex stands behind me, his hands resting on my shoulders.

I blink a few times, trying to figure out if I'm dreaming. Alex moved his things into my room over the weekend, and now I'm looking at his old room, except now it's been painted and filled with baby things.

The sea green walls are complimented by rich mahogany furniture. The crib sits against the wall, with a rocking chair right next to it. On the opposite wall is a dresser and changing table.

"I didn't choose any decorations, but I saw you eyeing this furniture set so I ordered it. And Emma showed me your baby board on Pinterest, I saw this color seemed to be a favorite." He's nervous as I step away, and look at everything more closely.

Turning to face him, I rush into his arms before I start to cry. "It's perfect."

He hugs me, his arms making me feel safe and loved.

"I love you, baby. And I love Little Bean, as you call him. I want to do anything I can to make you happy."

"Her." He laughs at me. "I love you too, Alex. I am happy."

He tilts my chin up with two fingers, swiping the tears off my cheeks with his other hand. "Me too. Happier than I ever thought was in my future."

Later that night, I can't sleep, so I make my way into the baby's room and start envisioning what it will look like once he or she comes.

Alex has been showing me every day that he is excited for this, but the work he put into surprising me with this room nailed it home. He wants this future.

When Dane and Emma moved quickly, I didn't doubt their ability to make it work for a second. But with my own relationship, part of me is still waiting for the other shoe to drop. I realize now that with Alex there is no other shoe.

Things may get rough, I'm sure we will face our fair share of issues, but I also know that we will work through them. I've always clung to the hope that someone would come along and sweep me off my feet. And that person is Alex.

Sitting in the rocking chair, I press my hand to my belly. "You have one incredible daddy, Little Bean."

I don't know how long I rock before Alex comes in to find me.

"You okay?"

Standing, I tuck myself into his side. "Never better."

"I'm going to be so huge for your wedding." I'm grumpy this morning. My show is in a week, and Alex and I argued about it again this morning.

"No, you won't. And even if you are, you're going to be

stunning. I promise." Emma hands me a cup of tea. I want coffee, but no one will let me drink any.

"I hate tea." She just smiles as I take a sip.

We're finalizing the plans for Emma's wedding, and it's dawned on me that I said no to Alex, so who knows how long it will be before he attempts to propose again.

"Everything is booked now. We've ordered what we need to turn the arena into a gorgeous reception area, and I've finally picked out your dress." She shows me a super cute strapless dress with an empire waistline.

Smiling, I hug her tightly. "I love it. Thank you for being so understanding."

"You're giving me a niece or nephew, that's the best wedding gift I could ever ask for."

We move to the couch. Sighing, I set my mug down. "Alex will probably never propose again. Not after I said no."

Emma laughs. "He's not going to give up that easily. I don't know what went through his mind those few days he was gone, but whatever it was, it settled any doubts he had about the two of you."

"I know that. I guess now that we've had a couple weeks to adjust, I'm more on board with the idea. At first I thought, 'oh sure, shotgun wedding.' Now, I realize I want it too. And maybe I jumped the gun to assume he was proposing for the wrong reasons." Okay, there is no maybe about it.

"I think that you need to stop thinking so much." She smiles knowingly.

Giggling, I nod. "Yeah, you're right." Pausing, I look at my best friend and future sister-in-law. "Thank you for reminding me to never lose hope. If I didn't have it, we wouldn't be where we are."

"Anytime. You were there for me, and I couldn't think of anyone better suited for Alex. It's one of the reasons I suggested he move here. Although, it took you longer than I thought to admit your feelings for each other."

A throat clearing interrupts our laughter. Looking up, we see Dane leaning against the kitchen island with a smirk on his face. "Sorry to interrupt, but Alex needs you in the barn."

Hugging Emma, I slip my boots on and make my way into the barn. None of the lights in the barn are on, but there is light shining from the arena. As I get closer, I realize they're flickering.

What is he up to?

When I step around the corner, into the open door of the arena, I'm stunned.

Lanterns are spread throughout the sand in a circle around a blanket that has a basket on it. Alex is nowhere to be seen.

The flickering light of the candles in the lanterns gives the arena a romantic glow. This is one of my favorite places to be in the entire world. Alex knows that, and now he's made it even more special to me.

I feel him come up behind me. The warmth of his body heating my back. When his hands land on my waist, I lean back and continue to look at what he's created from something so simple. I don't need flowers, or huge gestures. I love simple things that show me he cares and knows me. Everything in this room is something he dug up from the garage or the house, but with it he created something so romantic and sweet.

"I thought we could have dessert. This is about as close to a sandy beach as we will get for right now, but I think this fits you better than a beach anyways." Laughing, I take my boots and socks off walking towards the blanket. He follows me, sitting down behind me and holding me in his arms. His hands go straight to my stomach, cherishing me and the baby.

My stomach grumbles, so I peek in the basket.

Chocolate chip cookies.

"Oh my goodness. I've been craving these all day." Reaching forward, I grab one and take a bite. It's the perfect cookie, soft and chocolatey.

"I know. I saw the drool on your chin when Emma talked about baking some this morning." He takes the cookie I hand him, and for a few moments we enjoy them in silence.

After eating several, I turn to face him. He lifts my legs over his, his hands running up and down my thighs and calves.

Closing my eyes, I murmur my approval as he increases the pressure of his hands. The stroking becomes a massage, he's turning me into jelly. His hands fall away from my legs, a chuckle causing my stomach to clench.

"Baby, open your eyes." His voice is low, raspy.

When I do, he's staring at me intently. "Alex?"

"Lia, from the moment I laid eyes on you, I've been drawn to you. You make me smile in a way no one else can. You drive me crazy in the best way and, despite my best efforts, you found your way into my heart. I think in some ways I fell for you before anything even happened between us, but I was so guarded I didn't even realize it.

"You push me to open myself up. You've shown me that it's okay to entrust my heart to you, because in return you've done the same thing. I know you think it's too soon, but I disagree. I've been falling for you a little bit every day since I met you. You've given me hope for a future I never thought was in my reach.

"Now you've not only blessed me with your heart, but you're giving me the greatest gift I didn't even know I wanted. I love you. I've loved you longer than I realized, I think you knew how I felt before I did." He laughs, opening his hand. "Will you do me the honor of becoming my wife?"

The ring is a simple white gold band with two horse shoes

that form a heart. Small diamonds decorate each horseshoe. It's beautiful, simple, and completely unexpected.

Tears fill my eyes as I look up at Alex. He blinks away the sheen in his own gaze, watching and waiting.

"Yes."

One simple word. That's all he needed. He slips the ring onto my finger, before lowering me to the blanket and kissing me with a fierce passion.

"I love you."

"I love you too."

He holds his body over mine, pressing his hips into me. The intensity of the emotions running through me is overwhelming. I finally found my happily ever after. I just had to hold onto the hope that it would happen.

# EPILOGUE

*Alex*

Lia lopes into the arena, picking up speed as she races to the end and slides to a stop. Crossing my arms, I try to calm the beating of my heart. I'm pretty positive I'm the only person in this entire building who has a scowl on their face, but I'm pissed off that she's in there.

She's the most important person in the world, and she's carrying precious cargo, but there she is, competing at break neck speeds. I think she's going through the pattern at a speed faster than normal just to torture me.

"Breathe." Emma leans against the fence, her eyes following Lia through the pattern. "That girl could ride that horse backwards, with her eyes closed, and still win this."

"I know." I bite out. I do know. She's an incredible rider, and Ollie will always take care of her, but I still don't like that she's out there. "My baby is going to be on a horse before he's older than a day, isn't he?"

"She. And, yes, she probably will."

Emma and Lia are certain we're having a girl. I don't really care, I just like riling them up by calling the baby a boy.

"She's going to compete in the fall show too, isn't she?" Lia finishes the pattern, an elated smile on her face as she dismounts by the judges.

"Yep."

"There is no way I can convince her not to, is there?"

"Nope."

"Damn." Muttering to myself, I elbow Emma when she laughs.

"You better get used to losing these arguments, Alex. Lia was born to be around horses." Emma hugs Lia as she joins us outside the arena, before striding over to where Dane and Ryan sit in the bleachers.

"Great work, baby." My heart slows to a normal pace now that she's completed her last class. Wrapping her in my arms, I hold her tight.

She smiles up at me, her eyes shining from the thrill of the competition. "I love you."

"I love you too."

The End

You can read Ryan and Reese's story in **All About Forever** available now!

Sign up for my Newsletter: